A BACKWATER BLESSING

A GUARDIAN SECURITY AND A HEART'S DESIRE
CROSSOVER NOVELLA

KRIS MICHAELS

 Created with Vellum

This novella gives you the story of Cole Davis. You met Cole in Jasmine's book. For those of you who have read A Heart's Desire, this novella gives you insight on Agent Davis and may enhance Steele and Liam's story. This novella takes place as Joseph's book is playing out. I hope you enjoy it.

For those who might not have read the stories I mentioned above:

Joseph, The Kings of Guardian, Book Two

Jasmine, The Kings of Guardian, Book Six

A Heart's Desire - Steele and Liam's Story. A Stand Alone Novel

Story Description

When Cole, Mr. FBI, and Logan, local cop and reigning Ice Princess, hook up to solve a case of Mississippi corruption at the highest judicial levels, sparks fly. Their attraction is hotter than the sultry southern sun. She wants to hate him—but she can't. And Cole would never commit career suicide by staying in a backwater Mississippi town...not for any woman...especially not for Isabella Logan Church.

Excerpt:

The Fed had restraint. The question was how much? Deliberately she pushed her bikini clad breasts against his hard-muscled chest and lifted her hand to caress his cheek.

"If you are worrying about me being able to sell it...don't. I don't have to like you to act like I am making love to you." Her purred words sounded breathless and needy even to her own ears. She turned and walked out of the cabin before she did something stupid. Like crawl up his big sexy body and kiss him until his federal reserve broke.

CHAPTER 1

"This thing has all the hallmarks of a political nightmare."

Agent Cole Davis sat in Deputy Director Hayes' office and waited. Hayes paced, his shoulders hunched, as if the weight of the world pressed down on him. The furrows in the Deputy Director's brow lay in ruts, slashed deep and chiseled there by years of unrelenting stress.

Cole would do almost anything for the man. Hayes had been Cole's mentor since he stepped across the threshold into the agency. Green and wet behind the ears when Agent Hayes took him under his wing, the man became Cole's savior. Their student/teacher relationship had lasted through seven years and two promotions, which was amazing by Agency standards. He watched Hayes carefully, hoping his fast-tracking conclusions weren't the same as Hayes'.

"I need you to go to Mississippi."

Bull's-eye. Shit, why me?

"Mississippi?" Cole's voice didn't betray the emotion peaking under the false calm he projected. Damn it he'd proven himself—many times over. He was one of the best undercover assets in the Agency. Being sent on some podunk assignment to play nursemaid to a county sheriff was a gross misuse of his talent. He knew it and Hayes knew it too. But, if Hayes needed him...

"Listen, this isn't punishment. The contact I received this lead from is a friend. I met him at a Mensa convention about ten years ago." His boss scrubbed his hand over his five o'clock shadow and gestured toward the folder on the desk in front of him. "Look, a casual observer would never know it, but Kevin Deadeaux is a genius. His IQ is off the charts. If a fraction of what he believes is happening down there is, in fact, occurring, this assignment may be good for your career."

"May be?" Cole watched as Hayes stood and turned to look out the corner office window. He wanted a view like this. In fact, the drive he had to have his own corner office was the primary reason he'd consider taking this case.

"Taking down dirty federal judges will help to keep you highlighted for promotion. We're talking systemic corruption and graft. A deputy in Mississippi stumbled onto some information and has a theory. There is more than a possibility the deputy's instinct could be correct. If it turns out to be a wild goose chase? You did me a personal and professional favor. I'll owe you big time."

Hayes had always shot straight. If the man acknowledged he owed you a debt, it was a golden ticket. One he'd take. Cole digested the information and the promise. "When?"

Hayes tossed the slim manila folder toward him. "One week from tomorrow. This is your cover and a synopsis of my conversation with Deadeaux. Because of the federal implications, no one can know about your Agency ties. You'll go as a D.C. cop who wanted a change from big city crime. You were hired by the Lincoln County Sheriff's Department. You met the sheriff once through Logan Church, the deputy who put these wisps of information together. Your way past the good ol' boy system down there is through Church. You met each other at a hostage negotiation school the agency put on here two years ago. You kept in touch."

The director held up a hand stopping his question. "Yes, the class roster has been altered to show you both went through at the same time."

Reluctantly taking the folder, Cole asked, "What resources do I have?"

Hayes sat down in his chair and ran a hand through his hair. "Full support on all avenues, but you have to get us the evidence and information without the locals becoming curious. Kevin Deadeaux didn't go into details, but he's suspicious of everyone except Church. So, no contact with our local agents down there. We don't know how deep this stink goes, but from what Kevin insinuates, we could have dirt on multiple levels, local, state and most definitely federal. Dennison will be your contact up here."

Amber Dennison. Had Hayes purposefully sweetened the pot putting her on his team? The on-again off-again dalliance they enjoyed in the past might be on again. It didn't even bother Cole to think Hayes might know about their colleagues-with-benefits relationship. Hayes had a way of knowing everything. "Alright, I'll close out my reports and drift down south."

The director stopped him before he left the office. "Agent Davis, don't underestimate these hayseeds. They'll close ranks if they suspect you're a fed. Hell, the good ol' boy system down there would make the seasoned politicians in D.C. green with envy. I don't need you ending up dead."

Cole gave him a two-fingered salute on the way out the door. "Roger. I copy. Dying is not authorized."

The small cinder block building possessed two small windows. A neon 'open' sign flashed in one of them. It was the only sign on the building. How in the hell people figured out this was a diner was beyond him. The squat building beside Highway 90 could be anything, but his GPS indicated the neglected structure was Henry's Diner. The only customer in the place stood when Cole pulled the door open. He'd memorized Sheriff Deadeaux's picture, but since he was the only other patron in the roadside diner, the effort seemed meaningless. The man's wardrobe consisted of a 'Happy Hooker' t-shirt emblazoned with a huge fishhook, faded blue jeans and beat up white tennis shoes. He wasn't what Cole had been expecting. Yet the older man walked over and stuck out his hand as if they'd known each other for years.

"Damn, son it's been forever since I've seen you! I'm glad Logan talked you into moving south!"

Cole assessed the older man and relaxed. He slipped his practiced smile into place. With a long history in undercover work, adapting to his environment and the situation had become second nature. "Sheriff, it's great to see you again. I couldn't resist applying when Logan told me about the job opportunity. Thank you for taking a chance and hiring a city boy."

The two sat down as an overweight bleach-blond waitress sauntered to the table. Her yellowed nametag sat catawampus on her ample bosom. 'Selma' scratched her arm as she asked, "You need some more coffee, hon?"

Kevin lifted his cup and nodded. Cole turned a megawatt smile on the waitress. "A cup would be great. Thanks."

The old woman did a double take before she shuffled to the far end of the diner to retrieve the coffee pot.

Grabbing the opportunity, the sheriff lowered his voice. "We don't have much time because Selma will repeat everything she hears and make up what she thinks she's missing. She's a primary feeder conduit to all gossip east of the Mississippi River. We're having a quick cup and we're going to continue to act like we're old friends. When we leave, you're going to follow me to the marina. You got it, son?"

Son? The practiced charm Cole had been casting dropped instantaneously. "Let's be clear on a few points, sheriff. I'm here as a personal favor to the deputy director. I haven't decided if I'm staying. Until you brief me on everything you have on this case, my involvement is pending. I'll follow your lead—for now. And for your information, I am not now, nor will I ever be, your son."

The waitress started her return shuffle and both men leaned back in their chairs and smiled– two alpha males measuring each other under the pretense of friendship. She plopped down a new cup on the table, filled it and then topped off the sheriff's mug. She nodded at Cole. "So, you know Logan?"

The older officer chuckled to himself. Cole caught the sheriff's lifted eyebrow. The old woman had listened to their conversation when he'd entered the diner. He'd bet the diner was the perfect place to get or broadcast information.

"Yep, Logan and this guy met when they went to a federal hostage negotiation school in Washington D.C. a couple years back. Been keeping in contact since. Cole here used to work as a police officer in the nation's capital but decided to come down here and work with my department since the governor funded two more slots per coastal county. Got me a real steal this time, Selma."

The frizzed bleach-blond hair bobbed with her head as the waitress transferred her gaze from the sheriff to Cole. "Seems like it. You know this town. This one will put a few of those young women's tongues to wagging for sure. You say you're actually a *friend* of Logan's?"

Cole's eyebrow rose. The waitress' blatant hint all but implied Deputy Church didn't have a lot of friends. Screw it. Hayes had told him the way past the good old boy system down here was through Church.

The sheriff answered for him, "Yeah, Selma, I'd say they're very good friends."

The waitress cackled and fell into a coughing fit. When she recovered, she winked at Cole. "Yeah,

okay blue eyes, we'll go with that. Good friends…
with Logan. Honey, didn't anyone ever warn you
that's like being a friend with a 'gater? You're
asking to get bit. Good friends. Huh…well watch
your fingers. I do declare. I've got one to tell at the
next church circle." Her words faded as the woman
walked through the door to the kitchen.

Waiting for Selma to go far enough for them to
talk privately, Cole sipped his coffee. His face
twisted in disgust.

The sheriff snorted at Cole's grimace. "It's
Chicory."

"What?"

"The flavor in the coffee. We put chicory in it
down here. Local favorite. It's a taste you acquire."
The man across from him took a huge gulp of the
foul-tasting brew.

"I don't think so. Tell me I can get a normal cup
somewhere." The thought of going without a good
cup of coffee would be enough to tip the scales and
get him on the road out of this one-horse town.

"Yeah, you can. Ask for a regular grind next
time."

He motioned with his chin toward the waitress
who'd taken a seat at the diner counter. "It looks
like Selma took the bait, hook, line, and sinker. By

the time we get the boat out of the channel, half the town will know you're here." Two gulps drained his coffee cup to the dregs.

Cole pushed his full mug toward the middle of the table. That chicory shit was nasty.

"Come on. We have a full day of fishing on the agenda and Logan says they're biting hard and fast out past the Chandelier Islands."

Cole stood and threw five dollars on the table. Selma shouted from the counter where her cell phone was now glued to her ear. "Cops don't pay for coffee in here, honey!"

"Then you keep it, Selma, and buy yourself something pretty." Cole's smile and wink bought him a delighted cackle.

Cole followed the sheriff's cruiser down the deserted streets before they decelerated and pulled into a gravel lot. He parked and glanced around. The marina appeared clean with fishing boats lining about half of the sixty or so slips. Not one of the vessels was less than thirty foot long. No weekend pleasure boats either. These boats were serious fishing vessels. He stepped to the rear of his SUV and popped the hatch. Cole pulled a pair of flip-flops out, opened his suitcase and found a pair of board shorts.

He toed off his boots and jeans right there in the parking lot and slipped on his board shorts over his boxers. He left his t-shirt on and grabbed a ball cap.

The sheriff shook his head. "Regular chameleon ain't you, son?"

Cole shut the vehicle and locked it. Towering over the shorter man, he replied, "I'm damn good at what I do and once again—I *am not* your son."

The sheriff put a ball cap on his balding head and turned toward the pier. "Damn good thing… the next couple months might be awkward otherwise."

The sheriff turned and laughed, and Cole had a feeling he'd been made the butt of some private joke. Following the man down a well-maintained boardwalk, their goal became obvious—a fishing vessel moored at the end of the farthest pier. The *Backwater Blessing*, a fucking huge-ass, charter boat idled in its slip. Backwater Blessing? Really? As far as Cole was concerned, the only blessing he wanted was a quick bust of the dirty judges and then a fast escape, getting him the hell out of this backwater assignment. An engine door in the floor of the back deck was open, and a man wearing a life vest stood looking down into the gaping hole.

The sheriff hailed the man. "Hey Frankie! Engine problems?"

As the man turned around, Cole noticed the obvious Down syndrome traits. He was barefoot and wearing board shorts. He wore a yellow t-shirt with a huge smiley face on it.

"Hi Pawpaw. Logan fixed the engine. Said you was to put out to the channel as soon as you got on board with our new friend."

Cole walked up and held out his hand. "Hey, I'm Cole. Do you need any help?"

Frankie had a firm handshake. He squared his shoulders and proudly said, "Hi Cole. Nope, Pawpaw and I are good skippers."

The sheriff climbed the ladder and plopped down in the captain's chair. Cole watched as his new friend zipped his life vest and unlashed the moorings. He then carefully climbed up the ladder to the captain's console which stood at least fifteen feet above the deck and the cabin. The radar antenna started rotating when the engines engaged.

The shoreline slipped by as the boat moved toward the open expanses of water, and the sheriff moved over giving the young man the wheel. Cole watched the land disappear as the powerful boat sped south into the Gulf of Mexico. The ocean-filled skyline blossomed as the morning sun split huge white clouds with beams of red, orange and yellow. A view this tranquil was pretty damn amazing. Perhaps this assignment wouldn't be as miserable as he anticipated. *Yeah, right.*

CHAPTER 2

*L*ogan couldn't hear a thing. The roar of the diesel motors dulled to a din thanks to noise canceling headphones. She sat watching the repair and caught herself against the bulkhead when the ship lurched leaving the marina. No apparent leaks. A swipe of the rag against the back of the newly installed part came back dry. Thank God. Logan crab-walked to avoid smashing her head against the low ceiling of the below-deck engine compartment. She put away the earphones and placed the broken fuel pump on the deck. With practiced ease, she hoisted herself up and out of the engine compartment. Her lungs expanded welcoming the morning's cool fresh air.

The fuel smell from the repair had polluted the air in the compartment. Sitting on the deck with her legs still hanging into the bowels of the boat, she stared at the back of a large and amazingly well-built man. His thick brown hair flowed around his baseball cap as wind blew through it. The man stood watching the shoreline disappear. A beautiful sight to say the least. Not the shoreline…the man. He held his body tight against the motion of the sea and the drive of the vessel over the waves. Thick-corded ropes of muscle tensed and shifted in his back and arms. The wind plastered his t-shirt to his body showing off his tight waist that tapered to a fantastic ass and long legs. His calf muscles, cut and perfectly defined, stood in hammered relief as his body flexed, keeping him steady. If his lower legs were any indication, the man's thighs had to be a work of art. Damn board shorts.

Logan shook her head as she stood and wiped her greasy hands on a rag. *Holy shit, if his face is even halfway decent he's a twelve on a scale of one-to-ten.*

The thought dropped like a lead balloon. Not even a possibility. Even if the rest of the world was ignorant, she knew why the Fed was here. He wasn't a local and wasn't staying in the area once the case was done. He might be pretty to look at but being pretty was a fringe benefit.

Dismissing her thoughts as entertaining but idle speculation, Logan braced her legs against the weight of the hatch and carefully lowered it. The sucker was heavy and damned if her muscles didn't shake at the effort of closing the door without letting it slam. With the steel door finally lowered, she turned the key locks to secure the hatch to the decking. She stood up and stared directly into the coldest pair of dark blue eyes on the most handsome face she had ever seen...*crap and make him a fifteen on a scale of ten.*

Holy shit, if there is a God, please let the goddess on the deck be Logan. Logan? Where he came from Logan was a man's name. The curvy body lowering the steel hatch to the deck could never be confused for a man. Cole waited for her to straighten before he ran his eyes up and down her. She was amazing. No, amazing wasn't adequate. Phenomenal came close. He watched her eyes travel over him, imitating the head-to-foot sweep he had given her.

"Logan, I presume?" He shouted over the engine noise.

She nodded her head at him. "Cole, I presume?"

"I expected a man."

"Most people do."

Without waiting for a response, she tossed him a small smirk and turned away. He watched her curvaceous cut-off-clad ass scale the ladder to the captain's nest. Her long brown hair waved in the wind as she talked with the sheriff. The woman came back down the ladder, nodded toward the cabin and slipped through the hanging plastic strips that kept the air conditioning confined to the cabin.

"Pawpaw brief you on the case yet?"

Without the wind carrying her words away, her southern accent was instantly noticeable. And very sexy.

"What is a pawpaw?"

Logan's eyebrows popped up as if he'd asked a stupid question. "In the south, Pawpaw is slang for grandfather."

Cole did the math. The sheriff couldn't be more than sixty to sixty-five...unless he found the fountain of youth. "He must have married young."

Logan nodded. "Sixteen. He got Meemaw pregnant—rather scandalous at the time."

"Meemaw? You're shitting me, right?"

"No. It's what we call our grandmother. She was fourteen."

Cole snorted and shook his head, looking down to the galley floor. *Only in the deep, deep south.*

"Believe me, it happens in places other than Mississippi," she said.

Cole froze, his eyes darting toward her. *I didn't fucking say it.*

She continued to stare at him. "No, you didn't say it out loud, but admit it, you thought it."

Cole crossed his arms. His training engaged. She wasn't the hick he'd assumed. His interest kicked up another notch.

The glare she'd received in response to her taunt tickled her. People in his career field played mind games. Hell, she actually enjoyed the mental warfare, so she decided to show Mr. FBI Logan Church wasn't the push over he obviously assumed she was.

"Pretty serious over there Mr. Federal Agent. Are you trying to get a read on me? What can you tell?"

She soaped her hands over the sink and worked the lather to remove the stubborn grease and oil. Looking over her shoulder she gave him what she hoped was a dismissive look. "Do you have a type for me yet? Have you put me into a category?"

With her back to him, she continued to scrub the stubborn black film from her skin. "Do you think I am one of those cops pulling conspiracy theories from thin air?" She rinsed her hands and turned off the water. Reaching for a paper towel, she turned and leaned against the sink. Shaking her head, she continued, "I assure you, it's not the case. Oh, here's an idea. Maybe I'm a hapless hick. I got lucky and stumbled over the evidence." Logan purposefully put extra twang into her accent. "No, no…a bumbling idiot won't fit with the information you must have been given about the case."

Cole shifted his weight and straightened his

back. His expression remained completely blank. She raised an eyebrow and chuckled without any real humor. "Should I save you some time, Mr. Fed? I know my job. And surprise! I have the intelligence you assumed people around here don't possess. I'm a damn good cop and if you listen to the locals, one cold-hearted bitch."

L ogan bent quickly at the waist and flipped her hair over her head. The mass piled on the floor as she pulled a cloth elastic band off her wrist and secured the hair into a high ponytail.

She lifted up as Cole spoke, "Interesting diatribe. Since you've established what you are, what have you pegged me as?" His deep voice was dismissive and held a note of superiority.

Logan pulled off her white t-shirt. Underneath, she wore a navy blue and white striped bikini top. The top could be clearly seen under her soft white cotton tee, so his rapt focus on her actions amused her. She folded the shirt and put it neatly away in a small blue duffle. Finally, she responded to his question. "You, city boy, are a builder."

"A builder?"

Logan nodded and sat to take off her deck

shoes. "Yes sir, you're a builder. You're the type who will use this case and the rest of the cases you're assigned as a platform from which to springboard to deputy director or maybe someday director. People like you refuse to fail. You'll become whatever, and use whomever, to further your goals and maximize your gains."

Mesmerized by the waves of sexuality she exuded without any overt attempt, he breathed deeply and re-worked his initial assumptions. Her piercing grey-blue eyes registered as almost emotionless, cold as hell, and yes, he had concluded 'her highness' qualified as a bitch before she said the words. *Fuck, what did the deputy director get me into?*

The sheriff walked in the cabin and sat at the table. "Guess you want the whole story."

Cole leveled a blank stare at him.

"Son, your attempt at playing a statue has no effect on me. I'm immune. I raised Logan. You are minor league compared to her."

"Start with *her*. Logan is not a girl's name."

"*Her* is still in the room."

The older man chuckled. "Yeah, well it's *her* middle name. She won't let anyone use her first name. She and Frankie came to live with Cheryl and me after their parents were killed during a home invasion. We had the kids for the weekend. When we took them home, we found my daughter and her husband, tied, bound, and shot at point blank range. The crime is still unsolved."

Logan shifted and leaned against the counter in the galley.

The sheriff cleared his throat and pushed a thick folder toward him. "This is the complete case to include her notes and deductions. As you can tell by the volume of information in this file, I didn't tell everything to Deputy Director Hayes."

"Again, *I* am here. I *can* hear you."

The sheriff chuckled and tapped the folder. "Read it. We'll discuss the cover story if you choose to stay. If you want to pack it in and run, well, at least I tried. If I'm one hundred percent honest, I'll admit I'd like to walk away from what this folder holds. I can't. I *have* read Logan's report, and I *have* seen the suspicious trail of evidence. Logical conclusions based on the evidence can't be rationalized away. Look, if I hadn't made the damn call, sleep would have been a thing of the past. And damn it, I like sleep."

"You have friends in high places. Not many people pick up the phone and make a direct call to the Deputy Director of the FBI."

"You don't say?" He lifted off the seat and waited for Logan to pass him as they walked out of the cabin. Cole's eyes fell on the folder. Intense curiosity plus the thrill of a new case prompted him to open the cover. There was nothing like the rush of a new assignment. Even one in the middle of absolutely nowhere.

The boat slowed to an idle and he heard the anchor being lowered over the side. Cole glanced at his cell phone. He'd been studying the case file for over an hour.

Frankie popped into the cabin. "We're hooking red fish today. You like red fish?"

"Sure, they're good eating, right?"

Frankie nodded and smiled. "Yep, good eating." The young man grabbed four poles from the roof rack and headed out to the deck. Cole turned his attention once again to the folder. If he considered only the evidence, discounting the assumptions and the sound logical extrapolations proposed by Deputy Church, they had a thin trail to follow. He'd followed less and been successful.

Cole walked out on the deck. The heat and dense humidity of the Mississippi Gulf Coast clung to his body like a wet glove. He pulled his shirt off and put his cap and sunglasses back on. Frankie walked up to Cole with a baited pole. "Red Fish bite on squid. Can you cast?"

"I can. Thank you."

"You're welcome. I like this." He pointed to Cole's tattoo. Cole glanced down at the serpent on his right bicep where it wound through a skull. The diamond back rattler exited out one eye and then wrapped around his arm.

The young man traced the snake. "You're hard and you have big muscles—bigger muscles than Beau."

"I don't know Beau, but I have muscles this big because I work hard, like you."

Frankie thought for a moment before he smiled and cast his pole. "We work hard."

Cole launched the tackle and glanced from Frankie and the sheriff to Logan. She'd ditched her cut offs. The sun had turned her toned body a deep golden brown and *damn* how the woman rocked a bikini. Under the cover of his mirrored lenses, he surveyed her. Exceptionally long, muscled legs, tight high ass, tiny waist; flat, tight and toned abs and a rack he wouldn't mind getting lost in. As if reading his thoughts, she glanced over her shoulder and gave him a look capable of withering almost any man. He chuckled to himself and started reeling in his line.

They'd fished for about an hour before the sheriff threw a look at the agent. "You staying?"

Cole responded, "I am, but I'm following the tangible evidence and only the evidence."

Frankie chimed in, "Good! Evidence is your friend."

"It's a police officer's best friend." Frankie beamed at the sheriff's comment.

"Logan says, 'There is only evidence, Frankie, nothing else matters.'"

Cole studied Logan as she continued to reel in her line, seemingly oblivious to the conversation. "I think Logan is a very smart woman."

Frankie nodded, suddenly serious. "Logan knows a lot of things."

Logan cast a protective look at her brother as the sheriff set his pole down. "Frankie, would you please watch the lines? I need to talk with Logan and Cole in the cabin for a minute. Police business."

Frankie nodded, set his pole in the holder and walked to Cole, taking his reel. "Police business is important, Cole." Cole smiled at the young man and followed the others into the cabin.

The sheriff plopped down onto the bench seat on one side of the table. He took the bottle of water Logan passed him and downed it in a couple gulps. "Alright, you bought in, so this is how it's going to work. You two are an item. I don't give a shit how you sell it, but you sell it and sell it hard. The boys know you, Logan, and they know no local homeboy has a chance of getting your attention, not anymore. Cole, you're staying at her house with her."

He turned to Logan and emphasized, "People here have to accept him as someone who is here for the duration, someone who has a reason to stay here, part of the fabric. Any indication he's not here because of your alleged relationship and suspicion will run rampant. Those slimy sons-of-bitches will close ranks and this operation is over. Our only saving grace is those bastards feel confident, and they don't know we are on to them." The sheriff steadied a glance on Cole. "You have resources in Washington?"

"Full access. However, based on the initial report, it looks like we may need to get inventive on how we move evidence from here to DC."

The sheriff nodded. "We'll need to be careful with the chain of custody issue. If need be, you may have to take a trip back up north to settle business or tie up a few things because of your recent move...transport the evidence on your person. We'll figure it out when the time comes."

He turned to Logan. "He starts Monday. His uniforms, leather gear and body armor are in my trunk."

The sheriff picked at the rubber-topped table and added, "We'll transfer the equipment when we dock."

Shifting his attention, he pointed directly at Logan. "Honey, you need to lose the ice princess act and 'don't talk to me attitude' around him. Those men you work with need to see you two together and buy it. That's an order, not a suggestion."

Logan leaned back against the counter and smiled softly. "Alright, Pawpaw. I will act like a love sick puppy."

Her grandfather dropped his head into his hands and shook it slowly before lifting it. His gaze held hers. "Damn it, girl, nobody on the coast would believe you acting like a simpering idiot. Make it believable and make it happen."

The sheriff continued. "The way to unravel this is to get our information, locate witnesses and work the procedural evidence. We'll flip the low levels and sequester our witnesses, sheltering them from each other, the system, and ultimately, reprisal. You two will have to track down the leads and work it quietly. We will continue to coordinate outside work. Never come to my office with anything other than normal business and always bring a witness or make sure the door is open and every word of our conversations is heard. *Nobody* can suspect why he is here. Agent Davis is the lead on this investigation. His decisions dictate what we do, Logan. You got it?"

Logan gave a solemn nod, and with that assurance, the sheriff lifted off his seat and headed back out to the deck.

Cole watched the sheriff go with some misgivings and then turned his scrutiny to Logan. If the old man had to warn her to lose the attitude, could she handle the cover story? Was she capable of making the undercover operation look like a romance? Fuck. This case was probably damned from the beginning.

Logan lifted her eyes. Keeping her gaze on him, she walked across the small expanse and stood close—almost touching him. The combined heat and scent of their sun-warmed bodies sent a shiver through her. He stood at least six-foot, six-inches tall. She was five-ten, and he towered over her. He was obviously a bodybuilder. His huge chest, shoulders and arms made her feel tiny and...oh yeah...unbelievably alive. The air around them crackled with anticipation, and she could tell he felt it too. Her eyes dropped to his lips and lifted back to meet his eyes.

A single eyebrow arched, and a small smile tugged up a corner of his mouth. She leaned forward and brushed her lips against his softly. He held still, and his control won him some points in her book. The Fed had restraint. The question was how much? Deliberately she pushed her bikini-clad breasts against his hard-muscled chest and lifted her hand to caress his cheek.

"If you are worrying about me being able to sell it…don't. I don't have to like you to act like I am making love to you." Her purred words sounded breathless and needy even to her own ears. She turned and walked out of the cabin before she did something stupid. Like crawl up his big sexy body and kiss him until his federal reserve broke.

CHAPTER 3

The sheriff moored the boat in its dock effortlessly, manipulating the massive vessel as if it wasn't floating and drifting while it was being maneuvered. Logan took over and shut down the engines after the lines to the dock tied off. The trio had the end-of-trip clean up down to a science. Cole felt in the way and useless until he followed the sheriff to his cruiser and transferred his uniforms and gear to his truck.

"You got a piece, son, or do I need to get you a service weapon?"

Cole shrugged his shoulder and cupped the back of his neck thinking out loud. "I have my both my primary, a Glock 23, and my secondary weapon is also FBI issued. I'll keep them at Logan's. Better get me a service weapon so I can't be traced back to the Agency. And once again, I *am not* your son."

"Listen to me, Agent Davis, there are at least two sitting federal judges who have been implicated in some pretty serious shit here. If you believe Logan's informant, *and I do*, there is at least one murder and a cover-up. Work the facts and track the evidence. We are following your lead through this fucking mess. And for your information, you could do *worse* than being my son."

The older officer peered around the trunk lid and let out an ear-shattering whistle. Frankie hopped from the boat with a small cooler of fish and walked to the car placing it in the trunk. "Ready to go, Pawpaw?"

"You bet. Meemaw needs those fish."

Frankie turned to Cole. "Are you coming to eat tonight?"

He shook his head. "No, not tonight. I have to go unpack my things at Logan's house." The younger man seemed satisfied with the explanation and waved before he got into the car and again as the cruiser pulled away.

Cole walked back down the pier and watched as Logan finished buttoning up the vessel. "How long have you had the boat?"

Logan glanced over her shoulder at him as she fastened the snaps on the rain cover. "It was my dad's. He was a charter boat captain before he was murdered. The insurance paid it off and Pawpaw kept it up until he taught me everything there was to know about the Blessing. I take a few charters out on my days off. Pays for the upkeep and slip rental." Her voice and mannerisms held none of her earlier distant attitude.

She pushed the last snap together and turned around. Her hair was still pulled back in a ponytail and she wore a white t-shirt over the blue striped bathing suit top and her low-rise cutoffs. Those shorts were cut too high to be decent even with a swimming suit under them. Her skin had a dark rose color from the sun she had taken during the day.

Logan made a tsking noise and shook her head. "You're going to be sore tomorrow. You got too much sun."

Cole felt the tight pull and tingle of the sunburn. His abs and shoulders were bright red.

He shrugged and picked up his t-shirt off the deck chair. "Yeah, too much time in a suit. No worries, I usually tan quickly."

She nodded as her eyes focused behind him. "Shit. Looks like it's show time. Are you ready to start this charade?"

He put on his shirt and glanced at her. "Yeah, why?"

She nodded slightly toward the pier and the two men walking up the boardwalk. They were heading for the boat. *Time to start playing house.* Cole crossed the deck and took her into his arms. She leaned into him, and he kissed her softly. He pulled just far enough away to create the illusion he couldn't resist and then lowered his lips to hers again, parting them with his tongue. He explored her mouth and tasted her. Her scent and flavor, sweet and hot, intoxicated him. If not for the men behind them, he might have given into his baser desire to explore more than her mouth.

Logan's hands traveled up over his arms and shoulders and entwined in his hair. The bite of pain from his sunburn didn't diminish the attraction he felt. If anything, the sensation spurred his response. Cole pulled the elastic band from her hair, spilling the thick mass of brown waves around his arms and over her waist. Her body molded into him and his tongue slipped once again into her mouth and danced against hers.

A muffled cough sounded behind them on the boardwalk. He reluctantly pulled away from her. Putting his forehead on hers, he whispered, "Game time, baby."

She nodded, and he turned with her still in his arms. Logan's voice was cool and distant like it had been with him when they first met. "Cole, I would like you to meet two of the deputies from our department. Deputies Scott Ladner and James Saucier, this is Cole Davis."

Cole kept his arm around Logan and reached out with his right hand to make their acquaintance. "Nice to meet you."

The poorly veiled shock on their faces would have been funny if their relationship hadn't been a cover. But as the shocked look did relate to their cover, the response drew deep concern. Cole and Logan would have to work hard to make sure the pretense flowed.

"What are you two doing here?" Logan's question held no hint of warmth and only mild curiosity.

"Isn't it obvious? We came to meet the new guy.

Selma said he came in this morning before the sun was up. James, here, figured you were trying to hide him from us."

Cole laughed. "Sorry, nothing so diabolical. When Logan told me Frankie was expecting to go fishing today, I didn't want to screw his day up, so I drove through the night. I know how important keeping promises are for people with Down syndrome."

The blond man introduced as Scott seemed confused. "I don't follow."

Cole pulled Logan closer, and she leaned into him draping her arm around his waist and burying her fingers in the waistband of his board shorts. Both deputies openly did a double take. "It is quite simple actually. Some people with this particular disability can gain independence living their life by a schedule, and they count on that for normalcy and consistency."

The blond removed his ball cap and scratched his head. "Yeah, guess it makes sense. I never thought about it."

"Hey, Logan?"

"Yeah, Scott?" The sarcasm dripped from her voice.

The blonde continued, not put off at all by her

venom. "Janie and I are having a get together tomorrow night at our house. I know you don't usually come hang out, but the guys would like to meet Cole."

Logan's eyebrow rose as she stiffened his arms. Turning, she asked Cole, "You feel up to meeting everyone tomorrow night?"

She reached up and pushed his bangs out of his eyes. The act was intimate and sexy as hell. Those types of things would definitely sell their cover. Cole could see the deputies in his peripheral vision as they shot a quick what-the-hell look at each other.

"Sounds great. What time?"

"Seven. See you then?"

Logan nodded and asked, "What can we bring?"

James, the stockier man with brown hair, laughed. "Beer, what else?"

The two men shook Cole's hand again and walked down the pier casting backward glances every now and then. Logan slipped out of his arms and reached for her duffle.

"Grab the ice chest, will you?" She turned, lifted her eyebrows and in a saccharine tone called in a singsong voice, "Come on honey. Time to go home."

Cole chuckled and grabbed the huge chest full of ice, drinks, and fresh fish. His, "Yes dear," response won him a light and melodic laugh—the first real laugh he'd heard from her. Something told him those little outbursts were rare.

CHAPTER 4

*L*ogan let the agent she was supposed to be in love with into her home. She lived across the street from the beach, about three miles from the marina. The modest two-bedroom, two bath house boasted an expansive view of the Gulf. The view was the reason she'd bought it. Logan gave Cole the nickel tour. Darkening rays of deep pink and orange tinted by the sunset cast a hue over the furniture in her living room. A huge antique gun safe and a seventy-inch flat screen television hung over a massive fireplace garnered most of Cole's attention. Typical guy. She showed him the newly renovated kitchen. It had been updated but still appeared as if built a hundred years ago. Logan deviated from the tour long enough to pull a covered dish from the refrigerator and quickly shove it in the oven, cranking the temperature up. She led him upstairs to his room.

"The bathroom off the hall is yours."

Logan watched him as he walked to the windows and took in the last glimmer of the sun on the horizon.

"How did you know about people with Down syndrome?"

He didn't turn but talked instead to the window. "My niece has Down syndrome. She is the most honest, loving person I know. She has no defenses and no pretenses. She loves unconditionally."

Logan nodded as a knot formed in her chest. Emotion was not something she embraced easily, but his shared care of a loved one with Down syndrome struck a chord deep inside her—one she didn't want to admit. "I'm showering then heading downstairs to finish dinner. See you there."

Logan walked into her bedroom and closed the door, leaning heavily against it. The FBI agent had found her one and only weakness, her brother Frankie. With his quiet understanding, he'd effortlessly broken-down walls which had stood guard around her heart for years. Her mind raced as she tried to shore up defenses against the invasion the sexy agent probably didn't know he'd mounted.

Pulling herself off the door, she walked into her en suite bathroom, stripping out of the ocean-salt soaked clothes she wore. Turning on the shower, she stepped into the claw-foot tub and pulled the curtain around the antique porcelain masterpiece. Cool water poured over her as she tried to formulate a plan to deal with the relationship they would have to portray during the investigation.

Crap. How could she deal with the attraction she felt? It was obvious he felt it too. If he didn't, he was one hell of an actor. She'd be damned if she was going to get all googly-eyed over a man who wasn't going to be here a couple months from now. Still, everyone needed to believe they were a couple. How was she going to maintain distance from a gorgeous, dynamic, sexy man?

Her mind raced trying to formulate a situation where her two worlds, investigation, and cover story, would be mutually compatible. *Okay Logan, stick to the basics. Deal with the facts.*

Fact: He only wanted the advancement to his career this case could bring. He hadn't denied it when she had labeled him with it earlier. For that matter, he had stood impassively as she had accused him of it.

Fact: He'd be gone the second the case was closed.

Fact: He had her pegged as a bitch.

Fact: She'd avoided any type of personal relationship for the last four years.

And *there* was her solution. God knew she pushed the 'ice princess' persona to the limit with her co-workers, neighbors, and anyone else who wanted to get close. She'd be damned if she'd ever let anyone see her vulnerable again.

Logan did the wash, rinse, repeat thing and smiled to herself as the answer to her problem presented itself. When they weren't playing a couple, she'd treat him with the same ice cold distance as she did everyone else. Establishing it early, as in tonight, would set the tone.

L ogan peeked up from taking the cast iron casserole out of the oven as he came down stairs. Her brain blanked momentarily, before she nodded to a bottle of wine on the counter. *Wow.*

Just...wow. Thirteen...no fourteen on that ten-point scale. Damn, maybe she needed a new chart.

"Beef tips, cheese grits, roasted carrots, and biscuits. The wine is supposed to be a decent merlot. Would you open it, please?" *Sounded normal, right? Cool, polite...good.*

Logan turned her back to him, trying to push the image of the Adonis in her kitchen out of her head. His brown hair was still wet and tussled, his chin darkened with a five o'clock shadow and his chest, shoulders and biceps stretched his t-shirt to its limits. His jeans hung low on his hips encasing his muscled thighs and a fantastic ass. *Deep breath... dinner, yeah, continue with what you were doing.*

She turned back toward the Dutch oven holding the beef tips and grabbed the handle of the lid immediately searing the skin of her thumb and middle finger. The falling cast iron lid shattered the silence, crashing to the granite tiled floor. Logan hissed and spun around to the sink, slapping on the cold tap and shoving her hand underneath.

Beside her instantly, Cole grabbed her hand as she tried to pull it out of the water. "No, keep it under the water. The heat is still trapped under the skin. Cool it thoroughly before you bring it out."

Logan nodded as he held her hand under the stream. Her body clenched tightly from the pain radiating through her fingers. Vehemently she lamented almost to herself, "Of all the stupid idiotic things to freaking do. What in the hell was I thinking?"

She moved her fingers under the water and once again hissed in a deep breath. "Crap on a cracker! It hurts!"

He chuckled softly. "Then stop moving it." His massive body was hard against hers as he stood close and continued to hold her hand under the water.

Logan's head whipped around. She sent daggers in his direction. "Am I entertaining you?" His surprised dark blue eyes met her pissed grey-blue ones.

"No, Logan. Your pain does not entertain me. I was, however, amused at your exclamation. I can honestly say I've never heard, 'Crap on a cracker,' before."

He turned and reached for a dish towel on the counter and shut off the water. "Where is your first aid kit?"

She put her hand on the soft terry cloth. She

flinched at the pain screaming through her hand as she nodded toward a cupboard.

He opened the kit and took out ointment and bandages. "Come, sit over here and let me take care of your hand."

She walked to the kitchen island and sat on a barstool. He swiveled her chair toward him and moved so close his legs separated her knees. He blotted the moisture off her skin and held her hand close to his chest as he examined the blisters already starting to form. The sensation of his hands gently holding hers sent ripples of pleasure through her body despite the radiating pain from the burn. She drew a deep breath. His male scent surrounded her, the clean, fresh smell of his sham-poo...or was it his soap...Logan couldn't tell, nor did she care. Her body was committing treason against her brain's recent decree for cold detach-ment. Where in hell was her ice princess and frigid distance now? It was everything she could do to focus on her hand. Her mind imagined those amazing arms wrapping her...she breathed in sharply trying to stop her wild thoughts. The stupid ice princess had bailed on her. The bitch.

C ole applied a topical ointment to relieve the pain. He froze at Logan's gasp. "Did I hurt you?"

She lifted her face to his and he stopped breathing. Her thick brown hair fell away from her face and revealed full, red, heart-shaped lips. Her flushed cheeks and tear-moistened eyes revealed a vulnerability he wouldn't have guessed hid under all the layers of ice.

Logan licked her lips. His eyes followed her tongue. "No, please finish."

He waited, watching her breasts rise and fall as she tried to control her breathing. His body grew tighter against his jeans as he tried to discourage his mounting desire. The attraction sizzled between them, the currents almost visible...definitely tangible. Cole let go of her hand to open the band-aids. The minor task done, he turned back to her and sensed a resolve run through her. A curtain dropped. The minute crack hiding the tiny glimpse of vulnerability disappeared. Once again, the woman cloaked herself with the distance he had felt this morning on the boat.

After bandaging her fingers, he turned and put the kit away. "Take those off tonight when you go to bed to get some air to the blisters."

"Thank you."

He shrugged, "No problem. If you point out where the dishes are located, I'll get dinner on the table."

Logan sat at the island and watched as he set the table, opened the wine and served dinner. When he sat down, she cleared her throat. "You want to discuss this?"

This what? The sexual pull we feel? Hell, am I so transparent? Shit. Quickly deciding he wasn't going to be the first to talk about it, he turned and raised an eyebrow, waiting for her to continue.

"We need to discuss our cover. There will be questions we'll need to answer. But more importantly, we need to discuss the case in detail. I know how I would like to proceed, but I don't have your experience. Since you're in charge, I'll follow your lead. However, I know these people, and we need to proceed cautiously."

Oh, thank you, God. If he'd responded, he'd have looked like an idiot. He nodded as he took a bite of the beef tips and cheese grits. *Oh. My. God.* Cole closed his eyes as the explosion of taste hit his tongue. "Lord, this is not good."

Logan cast a glance from him to her plate, "What? Is the beef bad?"

"No, the food is fantastic. Which is the problem."

Logan's brow furrowed as she rubbed her temple with her good hand. "Excuse me?"

He filled his fork again. Damn, the flavors were beyond amazing. "I'm going to have to spend more time running. I could get fat down here."

Logan shook her head and chuckled without any real humor. "Thank you… I think. Anyway, I jog every morning. You're welcome to run with me, and the station has a decent gym. We all use it."

"Oh believe me, *it is* a complement. Your food is fantastic. I'll run with you in the mornings, especially if you continue to feed me like this. But you had concerns with the cover, and you wanted to run the details of the case. Which first?" He shoveled another mounded forkful of beef into his mouth as she took a drink of her wine.

"Let's talk about the case first. Okay?"

He nodded and stood. "Established facts." Cole walked back to the stove and ladled more food onto his plate. Damn, the woman could cook.

"Alright, I have a confidential informant statement that indicates the clerks of the district court are taking bribes to ensure certain cases are assigned to specific judges. A computer-generated randomized program assigns the judges' cases. The fact this process is being manipulated is concerning, at a minimum, and a reason to look deeper."

"Not to mention illegal."

"Right, so I looked. Based on the evidence, we can pull in the two clerks we know are manipulating the system and try to flip them. But until we have an iron-clad tie into the judges, I don't want to show our hand."

Cole leaned back in the chair and contemplated the information as he buttered a biscuit. "The association between the judges and the extended cases is flimsy at best. What evidence do you have to indicate their involvement?"

"Circumstantial. The sitting judges are hard-nosed and loved by the public for their hard stance on crime. However, I pulled all court decisions for the last three years and found a thread to follow. The cases manipulated by the clerks were juvenile females without parental involvement, so I started there. I searched all cases involving female juvenile offenders without parental involvement and found those specific cases were assigned to Judge Espinosa and Judge Sylvester."

"Interesting."

"It gets better. In each of those cases, no matter

the offense, the girls were remanded to court appointed custody and all the offenders were placed with the same core group of social workers. I couldn't go any further without getting a warrant to unseal the actual case files. All the information I have has been piecemealed together from documents outside those files. What I found supports my use of Amanda Bates as a confidential informant. After a troubled childhood, her parents washed their hands of her so, at seventeen, she had no adult involvement. She was remanded to a group home on a minor drug charge."

"But it isn't atypical for a remand to foster or group home for children without parental involvement." Cole scraped the remaining food from his plate with another biscuit. *Awesome cook.*

Logan emptied her wine glass and he refilled it for her. She took another sip and continued, "Yes, it is common. But Amanda alleges the group home is a front for a prostitution ring. I need to substantiate her information. According to her, the judges are feeding the pimps by picking the girls who can be manipulated and controlled. Amanda also told me one of the girls was beaten severely as punishment for noncompliance and died. She didn't know the name of the girl. Amanda said she was new to the home. There has been no report of a missing ward and there has been no body found. *If she is telling me the truth, it implicates the social services system or at a minimum one of the case workers.* I haven't looked into assigned case-workers yet because, once again, I need a warrant to unseal juvenile records."

"So, we are stuck between a rock and a hard place because we can't prove a murder if there is no body, no complaint of a missing person, or any evidence of foul play. I take it there are routine inspections done on the home and nothing is amiss?"

"Right. The group home is touted as the shining example of what all group homes on the coast should be. Amanda also said mass quantities of drugs and money pass through the home via couriers. The couriers and the bosses have meetings she is not allowed into. There are only a few girls allowed in. She alleges the judges are sometimes at those events. Of course, all of this is unsubstantiated testimony from a witness with a heavily checkered past."

L ogan finished her second glass of wine and watched as Cole opened another bottle, refilling both their glasses. The burns on her fingers had settled into a dull throbbing heartbeat of pain, but the wine created a pleasant warmth inside her.

"A huge problem with these allegations is Amanda's credibility. She has a history of lying to the authorities. How did she get you the information?" He finished his last biscuit as he asked the question.

"Her family used to live next to Pawpaw's when she was little. She knows Frankie and is nice to him. She passed a note to Frankie and asked him to give it to me. The note asked me to meet her before school in an alleyway she walks through from the group home. I have met her twice. To keep Frankie from being involved, we agreed if she needed to talk to me, she'd leave a blank piece of paper under a rock at the end of the alley. I check it every morning when I cool down from my run."

Logan watched him poach a forkful of the untouched food on her plate and pushed her dish closer to him. *This man was going to cost a fortune to feed. Maybe she could bill the FBI?* When he'd cleaned both plates, she carried her empty dish to the sink, as did Cole. After a quick cleanup, she grabbed the wine bottle before she walked onto the front porch. The moonlit view of the water gently lapping the beach had become a balm since buying the place. She turned on the porch ceiling fans but left the lights off. Cole joined her. They sat together on a large swing which hung to the left of the front door. She leaned over and put her wine glass on the white railing which circled the massive wraparound porch.

Cole turned to her. "We need hard evidence proving the judges' involvement. If we can't solidify the link, there's no way we can get a warrant. Right now, we have conjecture and the unsubstantiated word of a troubled young woman."

Logan sipped her wine and nodded, focusing on the water. "I've been thinking about how we can work it. Obviously, putting an undercover agent in the group home as a social worker wouldn't work. It would take too long to get an agent into the good graces of the group home management. And we can't work it from the other open avenue. Let's face it, not many cops can pass for a juvenile, and if anything, Amanda told me is true, she may be forced to work clientele."

They sat in silence. The only sound was the repetitive gentle swish of the water hitting the sand.

He drew a deep breath. "Then we work the only other angle. We infiltrate the drug operation, bring down the prostitution ring and work the threads back to the judges. The FBI has under-cover agents and private assets in various drug cartels. If those ideas don't pan out, I can contact the Agency to see what visibility they have on the situation. I'll need to reach out to my people. If we can connect an active operation in the southeast to the one we are investigating here, we can establish credibility for your witness. Her information will allow us to track the drugs or money and work toward the judicial implications. I'll need to release the information on the group home. It wasn't in the original report."

"Because of the lack of credibility of Amanda, I redacted it. I believe her, but I wasn't sure if you'd be willing to. Anyway, the scope of the operation you're proposing means we'll need to include other people. How can we maintain our cover?"

Cole stood and walked to the railing taking the wine bottle and filling both glasses again. As he sat down beside her, he shrugged. "We may need a lawyer to work with us to substantiate the evidence against the clerks but the need for a lawyer will be toward the end of our efforts. The FBI works closely with an agency that has resources you wouldn't believe. We can get access to a lawyer who has been vetted at a higher level then you or I will ever reach. My agency will probably supply the undercover agent for the drug angle unless the DEA throws a fit. Warrants will need to be at a federal level, so my people will work them. We can't risk alerting the lower courts here. The biggest logistical issue will be how we request and receive information from D.C. Personal courier would be best as phones and computers are easily monitored and compromised. We can work it as it becomes necessary. I assume my communications aren't suspect, but I don't want to take any chances. I'll buy a burner phone for my calls to Washington. I don't want to risk bringing anyone in until we must. We need to keep a tight lid on this."

Logan chuckled softly, "No worries about me saying anything. I hardly ever talk to people anyway."

Cole pushed the large swing they were sitting on with his foot and started it rocking. "Why?"

Logan lifted her shoulders and sighed. "It's the way I am." *Translation: Not going to bare my soul to you Mr. FBI.*

"Alright, let's discuss the cover. We met two years ago at a hostage negotiation school we both attended in D.C."

"Yeah, we hit it off and have been meeting over long weekends and holidays. Nobody here tracks my free time and I don't associate with them off duty. Claiming to have a long-distance relationship with you won't raise any warning flags."

"We need some depth and details to make it believable. I need basic information, your full name, birthday. Some superfluous stuff so we can act like we actually know each other."

"Easy enough, my full name is Isabella Logan Church. I'm twenty-seven-years old and I was born August 4th. My favorite color is red. I'm addicted to cheese popcorn and I have yet to find a food I don't like...although snails are close to inedible. I work out religiously and run every morning unless I'm taking the boat out. The boat, by the way, is my hobby and my favorite pastime is music. Your turn."

He whistled. "Isabella?"

She nodded.

"Cheese popcorn, huh?"

She laughed softly. "Yeah, now your turn."

"Cole Ryan Davis, I'm thirty-five-years old. I was in the Marine Corps before I joined the agency, or should I say the police force, in D.C. My birthday is April 12th. My favorite color is blue and I'm a meat and potatoes kind of guy. Don't like fancy food on tiny plates. I'm addicted to the gym, weight lifting specifically, and I run but only because I am a meat and potatoes kind of guy. My favorite pastime is sports, any sport at any time, but I am a football fanatic, both college and professional."

"Roll Tide? War Damn Eagle? Hotty Toddy? Geaux Tigers?"

He almost snorted the wine he was drinking.

"Hell no, definitely not. Michigan, the Big House. Go Blue, I'm a Big 10, SEC-hating purist."

"You are going to have some fun down here in the wilds of SEC country."

"Don't I know it."

He turned to her and asked, "What type of music?"

She smiled in the dark. "Anything I can play on the guitar, not that I am going to be playing for a couple days." She drank the remainder of her wine and held up her hand looking at the bandages on her fingers.

"Does it still hurt?"

"Yeah, I can feel a throb, but the wine has definitely dulled it." She turned to face him bringing her legs up and hugging them against her chest as she let out a small sigh. "Cole, I have a confession."

He turned in the seat and put his arm on the back of the swing, his hand playing with the long brown hair spilling over the cushion. "What's your confession, Bella?"

He could see her beautiful face in the moonlight and watched as she closed her eyes. "Uh, honestly, don't call me Bella. Anyway, I need to tell you this because it is imperative we appear as a couple to everyone."

Cole's fingers stopped playing with her hair. His mind was instantly sharp. *God, please do not let this woman be gay.*

She opened her eyes and pinned him with an intense stare. "I have never had a successful relationship."

He waited, expecting her to say more, but she didn't. He took a deep breath and asked, "Why?"

Logan shrugged and laid her head on the cushion trapping his fingers. "A myriad of reasons. I have no idea how to act with you because I have next to nothing to base the cover on. The bravado and the scene on the boat today notwithstanding, I'm drifting on the waves without an anchor when it comes to doing this."

He cupped her cheek with his hand. Logan pulled away immediately. He chuckled. "No problem. You did well this afternoon. Don't worry. We can make it work. Follow my lead. Smile at me when I talk to you and don't pull away when I touch you. I can do the rest."

"I'll do my best and please don't call me Bella."

She got up out of the swing and stretched. "I am running at six before it gets too hot and muggy. See you in the morning."

"Logan?" She stopped and waited for him to speak.

"I have no problem with this cover, but it is only a cover. We both have a life outside this operation and we'll both go back to it when the case is done."

He watched her ice princess attitude return in

all its glory. She turned and arched an eyebrow in a regal gesture.

"I never doubted it for a second, Cole. My focus is on this case and only this case. I told you what I did about myself to ensure our cover was believable. If you imagined anything else, you were in error."

CHAPTER 5

*C*ole sat on the porch enjoying the sound of the water lapping at the beach. The sun sank on the ocean's horizon. All in all, it had been a good day. Cole ran five miles with Logan this morning and then they went their separate ways for the day. He bought a burner phone and made some calls starting the process of requesting assets to work the drug angle. He briefed Deputy Director Hayes on the entire case and checked in with his parents.

With those mandatory items out of the way, Cole drove around the arca and explored some of the coastal towns. Mississippi's sixty miles of coastline took less than an afternoon to traverse, even after stopping at several local establishments. He'd made it back about an hour before they were to leave for the party. Showered and changed into jeans, boots, and a white polo shirt, he wandered downstairs to wait for Logan. She'd gone shopping and stocked her industrial sized refrigerator. Pulling a soda out of the door, he popped the top and sipped it while he lazed on the porch swing watching a shrimp boat pass by on its way to the marina.

When she appeared on the porch, it was as if someone had forcibly sucked the air out of his lungs. How this woman had never had a long-term relationship was beyond him. Tan and sultry, the woman exuded sensuality. He closed the distance between them, lifted her chin and smiled. "From this point forward we're a couple, unless we're inside and alone. Then, and only then, can we be ourselves. Follow my lead and don't act any different to others than you normally would. I am your world. I am the only one you act differently toward, and if you can handle those restrictions we are solid."

"We're solid. I got it." He leaned down and brushed his lips against hers softly. "Let's go play house, Bella." He grabbed her hand and walked to his vehicle, opening the door for her.

"Would you please stop calling me Bella?"

"No." He winked at her as he started the SUV. He laughed at her angry growl.

The drive to Scott and Janie's was short, only about ten minutes, but the tension in the vehicle grew as they searched for a parking place. Cars lined the street and if that was any indication, the party was well attended. Logan closed her eyes. "Every damn one of them is here, and ten bucks says the ones on patrol rotate through to meet you."

"Is it a problem?"

"I'm not comfortable around crowds. I've been told my manners suck."

He shrugged. "Let's get it over with. I have no problem meeting people. I'll be charming enough for both of us." He got out of the SUV and walked around to her door as she was getting out. People inside the house didn't hide the fact they watched as he pulled her into his arms. "We have an audience Bella, now be a sweetheart and reach up and put your arms around my neck."

Logan slid her hands up his biceps and entwined them around his neck.

He bent down and brushed his lips against hers as she leaned in. "Now smile at me and take my hand, remember you don't have to be different with them, only with me."

"I'm not stupid. I understood your instructions the first time, and don't call me Bella." The saccharine coated words dripped from her smile. He laughed and grabbed her hand, purposely not paying attention to her inventive grumbling. They walked to the back gate. A mass of people immediately enveloped them.

Logan introduced him in her typically cold and distant manner. Her demeanor matched what it had been on the boat the first morning. Cole accepted a beer but kept his hand entwined with hers, careful not to touch her bandaged fingers.

Citronella candles burned atop five-foot stakes positioned around the yard keeping the gnats and mosquitoes at bay. A crowd of people stood interspersed around picnic tables strewn with food. Those not eating stood visiting, and most of the officers surrounded him and Logan. She'd done well handling the attention and his constant tender touches. She remained quiet, but he assumed quiet was her natural demeanor. Responding to his caresses and initiating a few of her own raised eyebrows and earned more than a couple comments sent their way.

Leaning up to his ear, she whispered, "If you don't let my hand go, you will have to accompany me to the bathroom."

He beamed a smile and pulled her close, kissing her soundly and whispering against her lips, "Hurry back." She smiled and peeled away from him, heading toward the house.

The deputies Cole spoke with kept up a light-hearted banter of mutual harassment. Normal ball busting for cops, no matter the department. He had no problem fitting in and feeling comfortable. Accepting another beer, he caught movement out of the corner of his eye. A young and obviously drunk man walked, or rather staggered, up to the group. He motioned toward Cole. "Dude, did you know you screwed up the running bet we have at the station?"

Cole twisted the cap off his beer. "Really? How's that?"

"Man, we figured for sure the woman was one hundred percent dyke. Every man on every force plus everything with a dick in the coastal fire departments has tried to hook up with her, but she's like a freaking ice fortress."

Cole gave the drunk man his full attention. In a reaction to the homophobic comment and the insult to Logan, his body stiffened. He sat his nearly untouched beer on a nearby picnic table. He felt the other deputies back off. Cole assumed they waited, assessing his actions, ready to react if needed.

"Exactly how long has Logan been a target of every man on the force?" The question came out in a possessive growl, but the alcohol-soaked brain of the newcomer didn't recognize the warning.

"Man, I don't know? I know guys who have tried to get in her pants. She's turned everyone down and busted balls in the process. I mean, she is frigid. You could freeze water on her ass." The drunk snorted at his own joke.

Cole's eyes narrowed. "So, what you're telling me is every man on this force has been hitting on my woman?" Tension encompassed the area immediately surrounding Cole and radiated outward, silencing the people immediately adjacent to their small group. The backyard crowd shifted as deputies put down beer bottles waiting to see what Cole would do. The drunk, however, was clueless and laughed, elbowing Scott, their host, who'd walked between the two men.

"Yeah, it was fun setting up the newbies to be shot down by her. Freaking disaster, real life crash and burn episodes, yah know? Like watching a gnat getting zapped by a bug light. One look at her will make you burn so freaking hot and then she's ice cold."

Cole tensed and took a step toward the idiot as Scott stepped up blocking his way. "Whoa, Cole, he didn't mean anything by it."

The drunk gaped at Cole as if he'd been struck. "What the fuck, man? What did I say?"

Cole lurched at the fool. Scott's solid body blocked his way. The asswipe deserved a beat down. He reached over Scotts' shoulder, taking a swipe to try to reach the waste of sperm. "You stupid son of a bitch, you blatantly disrespect the woman I love, and you expect me to be good with it? You ignorant moron! She's a cop who'd take a bullet for you. She'd back you up in a deadly situation, and you think it's alright to harass her and make her the target of your fucking games?"

Scott leaned his weight into Cole and pushed him back separating the two men further. "No, man! Hey, we don't. Curtis here, he's one of a few who doesn't get Logan. Everyone assumed she had someone. She had to, man. I mean, she never went out, and she never encouraged any of them. Not after Beau. No one got in her face. I wouldn't allow it. She's one of the best. We'd all take a bullet for her, man. Don't listen to him. He's had too much to drink and well...dammit, he *is* a fucking moron."

Cole peeled his eyes away from the deputy escaping through the crowd and took a scant second to glance at the man who still held him back. Cole relaxed slightly and lifted his arms up in surrender, stepping back. His eyes latched back on the inebriated jerk who retreated from the gathering.

Scott handed Cole his forgotten beer and changed the topic. "Minus the drunks, how do you like Mississippi, Cole?"

A long draw on the beer gave him a moment to cool down. The asshole had lit his fuse and surprisingly he'd acted like a lovesick fool. *WTF?* Well, it worked for the cover. Yeah, he'd go with that explanation. Cole lifted the beer in a salute. "For the most part I am enjoying it, with the obvious exception."

Scott laughed nervously. "He's a jerk, and he has a lot to learn."

Cole glanced toward the house, watching Logan walk down the stairs. Scott followed his gaze. "You plan on sticking around, I mean, with her?"

Cole turned his attention back to his host and let a smile play across his face. "Yeah, I am. Hey, listen, man, I'm sorry about the scene. It's… well…" Cole stopped when he realized he actually had no idea how to finish his thought without sounding like a chick with a dick. Finally, he shook his head and said, "That shit's not acceptable."

He glanced over at Logan as she crossed the backyard and walked up to him. "I'm here for good."

He lifted his arm as she stepped next to him and tucked her close. She ghosted a smile at him and took a beer from Scott.

"That's the nicest thing I've heard since break-fast this morning." With her free hand, Logan reached up, fixed his collar and slid her hand down his back, putting her unburned fingers in his back pocket.

A little pixie of a blonde had followed Logan out of the house to the gathering. She put her arm around Scott, who threw an arm over her shoulder as she asked, "Oh, and what did you hear at breakfast?"

KRIS MICHAELS

Cole threw back his head and laughed. "Sorry, I'm not repeating those comments in public."

The woman held out her hand and introduced herself. "Since my husband has failed to do so, let me introduce myself. I'm Janie Ladner. Logan and I actually happen to be distant cousins." Logan stiffened slightly in his arms as Cole extended his hand toward the woman.

"Good to meet you, Janie. Thank you for inviting us tonight." The petite blonde smiled invitingly and ran her eyes up and down Cole. "You're most welcome."

He caught the sexual overtone and ignored it, instead dropping his gaze to Logan. He lowered his lips to hers, grabbed a handful of her hair and cupped her neck. He lifted his head and considered the little blonde.

"Since it's only my second night here, I think we'll call it an early night. No offense, but having her alone for more than a short weekend? Well, I hope you understand." He dropped his gaze to Logan. "Isn't that right, Bella?" Logan nodded.

"Bella? You haven't allowed anyone the use of your first name since your momma and daddy died. He really must mean something to you. Guess Cole is someone I should get to know better." Janie's double meaning made a few people clear their throats. Cole pretended not to notice and pulled Logan with him as he drifted toward the gate.

They spent the next twenty minutes saying goodbyes and extracting themselves from the gathering. When he finally opened the backyard gate, Scott followed them.

"Cole, I want to apologize again for earlier. The kid's a moron, and I know he'll regret what he said when he sobers up."

Logan stopped short and whipped her head around. "Who? What? Who said what?"

Scott snuffed out a laugh and shook his head nodding toward Cole. "He'll tell you after you leave. I don't want you going back there and kicking anyone's ass. I know you. You would."

Scott pushed her up into the SUV, shut her door and leaned against it, ignoring Logan's irritated mutterings.

"The sheriff asked me to be your training officer for the next couple weeks. I know you don't need any law enforcement training, but I can show you the ropes in the county. Naturally, you can't ride with Logan since you're involved. We're all working the same shift, so you can ride with me until you're comfortable with the patrol area and our routine."

Cole nodded. "Thanks, I appreciate it. Tell the drunk asshole to steer clear of me. It'll take a while for me to get over being as pissed as I was tonight. I don't think I'll be sharing a beer with him for quite some time."

Scott nodded and walked away. Cole maneuvered the SUV away from the curb. Logan turned her head toward Cole. "What did he say?"

Cole shrugged. "Said everyone thought you were a lesbian and it was fun to watch you bust balls on the guys who tried to ask you out. Scott said he knew you had someone on the side."

Logan turned toward the passenger window as they traveled, and Cole wondered if her co-worker had hit the nail on the head. Cole glanced at her. "Did you? Have someone on the side?"

She shook her head, continuing to gaze out the passenger window and replied, "Nope. No one. Not a flippin' soul. Nadda, zip, zilch, no."

Cole laughed. "Methinks the lady doth protest too much."

Logan turned and smiled. "You believe what you want. By the way, the jealousy thing...telling whichever asshole it was to stay clear? The possessive attitude will sell well down here, but in case you get the idea I need a knight in shining armor… I don't."

"There is absolutely no doubt in my mind you can take care of yourself."

CHAPTER 6

*C*ole popped a beer and settled in to spend some quality time in with Logan's seventy-inch flat screen. The only problem with this scenario? At ten o'clock on a Saturday night, there isn't shit on television. A quick run through the channels left half a bottle of beer and absolute boredom. A couple swigs later, he headed upstairs. The sound of a shower running removed any doubt about what Logan was doing.

Cole's insides itched. He was strung tight. Screw it. A shower might relax him enough to get some rest. A quick right turn put him in the bath-room. The shower wasn't huge but it was better than a lot of accommodations he'd used while undercover.

The hot water felt good, and the shower massage pulsed with fair to decent pressure. White noise blanketed out the rest of the world. Images of the stupid fuck who'd insulted Bella flashed, sending another jolt of pissed off through his body. Not like him to be a caveman. He'd worked tight undercover operations with what…at least four other female officers. He'd never reacted to a situation emotionally, and he'd been in plenty of tense situations before. What the hell was his issue with her?

She's a cop working a case. It shouldn't matter if she's female. A smoking hot female, granted. He palmed a handful of body wash. Those kisses and touches tonight had smoldered with a sizzling heat. His cock twitched and came to life thinking about the woman's scent, the way her body fit perfectly against his side. Damn he'd bet she was a hellion in bed. He imagined she'd be wild to fuck. She wouldn't—*shit!*

The falling water turned from fantasy warm to arctic cold in less than a second. Cole rinsed hastily and practically fell out of the shower. *Note to self, do not shower at the same time as Logan.* The freaking hot water heater couldn't handle it. When his heart finally started beating at a normal tempo, and the icicles that hung from his flash-frozen balls melted, he dried and wrapped a towel around his waist. Halfway across the hall he stopped, remembering his dirty clothes.

Turning to retrieve them, he paused at an indistinct sound. What had he heard? He held his position listening to the unfamiliar creaks and groans in the little house. There…there it was again. Cole padded back toward the end of the hall. The small sound beckoned him farther. A stilted moan drifted toward him from Logan's room. He lifted his hand to knock on her door but stopped short when he heard a hissed intake of breath.

Cole pressed closer to the door, listening intently. A steady humming suddenly broadcast through the silence. Her low groan and the creak of bedsprings froze him. Son-of-a-bitch—a vibrator! Cole leaned his head against the doorjamb. His cock stood at attention and wept at the mental picture of her spread eagle on her bed, naked and using a vibrator. He reached down and gripped the base of his dick through the terry cloth of his damp towel. His hips bucked against the friction. Logan gave a breathy moan and he lost it. The towel dropped, and he grabbed his cock with one hand and his balls in the other. The vibrator's volume rose and fell. She had to be stroking inside herself. Fuck, he wanted to see her sex spread and weeping for him. He wanted to be tasting her, licking and sucking her clit while her body writhed beneath him. His hand jerked up and down his cock aided by copious amounts of precum. He bit his lip when he heard the springs of the bed start to sing in a subtle rhythm. Fuck, her hips were bucking. He could see her tanned body, tight with a slight sheen of perspiration. Her nipples, God what color would they be? Dark rose or maybe light brown and tight. Fuck yeah, they'd be hard as pebbles. Taking those buds with his lips, he'd nibble at them until she arched against him and…

Her heavy gasp and low drawn out moan pushed him over the edge. He pictured her body in the throes of orgasm, clenching around his cock. His balls drew up and exploded. It was everything he could do to keep silent as his orgasm tore ropes of cum from him. He could hear her panting as he held onto the oak of the doorjamb struggling to keep silent while listening to her gasp for air.

Finally, able to open his eyes, the white streaks of cum dripping down the wall slammed him back to reality with a thud. *Damn. Psycho much?* Cole drew a quiet breath and reached down for the towel on the floor. He cleaned away the evidence of his audio-voyeurism and carefully crept down the hall. The floorboard outside the guest bedroom creaked under the weight of his foot. Cole bolted into the room. He was under the covers before he heard the door to her room snick open. *Fuck!* He hadn't closed his door. Dropping an arm over his eyes, he strove to regulate his breathing. He heard her walk down the short hall and pause at his door. She lingered for a moment before descending the stairs. Small sounds from the kitchen echoed in the stillness of the night.

Jesus, he'd never done anything like that before. When the cold water blasted him, his brain must have shriveled as much as his dick. Cole rolled to his side and took note of the almost full moon framed by the bedroom window. People did crazy shit during full moons. He'd been a cop long enough to know it for a fact. *Yeah, Davis, blame it on the moon. Moron.* Listening intently to the small sounds the house made as she walked through it, he tracked her until she passed by his room again. Her pause and light sigh brought a smile to his lips, although it shouldn't have. The chemistry between them was explosive. *Like a fricking ten-pound brick of C4.*

The last three weeks had been an exercise in patience. The case had been frustratingly slow to develop. The evidence he and Logan followed pointed toward a tie between major drug traffickers and high placed local political and judicial appointees. Right now, all the evidence was circumstantial, but he'd organized a meet with an undercover DEA agent next week. He hoped to tie the players he and Logan had identified to a Federal DEA case. A multijurisdictional effort would increase the chance of their discovery by either the drug traffickers or the dirty politician and judges, but with the amount of evidence he and Logan were amassing it was a risk they'd have to take. They needed more manpower and adding another agency was their only viable option.

Entering the flow of traffic on I-10 East, Cole chuckled to himself as all the NASCAR wanna-be's slowed to seventy miles an hour. Blue lights and a shield on a car immediately transformed lead feet into law-abiding citizens. He settled into the far left lane and headed back to the station. He was happy, which was…well, it was strange. He and Bella had developed a friendship while working the case. He didn't have to act at being her significant other. If it wasn't for his training and the fact he'd be leaving when the assignment was over, he'd break down the fragile barrier keeping him from her bed. But the barrier kept the public caresses and kisses from becoming a private matter. He wanted her. She couldn't hide her body's response to him. She was adept at working out her frustrations behind closed doors. He kept his open and listened for those nights. Damn, he was so screwed.

Cole cranked the air conditioner and floored the accelerator to break through the gaggle of speed-limit-respecting drivers on the interstate. After their shifts, he and Logan worked out together at the county's gym. He was popular with the other officers, making friends and fitting in. Logan watched quietly and kept her distance, not changing her usual behavior with anyone but him. The sexual tension between them validated their cover story. Not that any intel had implicated her co-workers, but until they knew for sure how deep the corruption ran, he and Logan would be forced to keep up appearances. He wasn't complaining. Nope, not at all.

When he entered the gym, three men he didn't recognize loitered at the door to the cardio room. The men obviously didn't see Cole walk up behind them. He glanced past them and stopped dead in his tracks. There were two machines in use and the fifty-year-old dispatcher wasn't the one attracting attention. No, the men drooled at Bella's heart shaped ass as it rhythmically gyrated while she pumped through her workout. The effort it took to climb the imaginary ladder she currently ascended coated her and her sports bra in sweat. The sheen on her skin accentuated the toned muscles of her legs and lower back. Her nipples pushed hard against the damp material leaving nothing to the imagination. *Holy shit.* Clearing his throat, he caught their attention and nodded. The largest of the three nodded back.

Cole made a motion toward Logan and asked, "You know her?"

The officers chuckled, and one responded, "Yeah man, she's a deputy sheriff. You must be one of the new highway patrol hires?"

Cole's eyebrows shot up. He wore plain grey

workout clothes. They wouldn't be able to ID his organization.

The middle of the three added, "Yeah, I could stand here and watch her ass all day. She's definitely ten pounds of sugar in a five-pound sack."

The third man elbowed the one talking. "Dude, didn't you hear? She has a man."

The first man pulled his hands through his dark brown hair. "Who, Beau? That fucker's long gone. Stupidest son-of-a-bitch on the face of the earth. Who'd leave her?"

"Nah, I heard it was some city cop moved down here to be with her."

"Some pansy ass from the city? Like a city boy would be man enough to straddle her wild piece of country ass. She needs a fireman. We have better hoses."

The men laughed at the joke. Cole fought down the urge to choke the shit out of them. He pushed past the firefighters and headed toward Bella before he did something he'd regret. Eyes closed, she listened to her iPod. He knew the assholes were watching him. Cole softly tugged the wire connected to her ear buds. Beautiful grey blue eyes popped opened. The smile on her face? He hoped he was responsible for it.

At a crook of his finger, she bent toward him. He kissed her, pulled back and smiled. She winked at him, closed her eyes and continued her work out. Oh, no. He'd missed his workout time, so she needed to be done too. *Fair was fair. Besides. Dinner. Damn the woman could cook.* Cole laughed at his own motives and walked behind the machine lifting her effortlessly off the apparatus. He tossed her over his shoulder like a rag doll. She shrieked in surprise and every head in the gym swiveled and stared their way.

"Cole Ryan Davis, put me down this instant!" Logan dangled down his back and slapped his ass when he adjusted her on his shoulder. He laughed at her efforts and held her legs with one hand while he tickled her mercilessly. Her giggles and shrieks echoed throughout the gym. As he passed the men at the door, his gaze dismissed them. "Don't worry y'all, this city cop is more than enough for her."

Cole carried her out of the building still tickling her. Logan had only one option to get his attention and damn him if she didn't use it. She pulled the waistband of his shorts out, stuck her hand down and grabbed his ass cheek. The shock of her uninhibited behavior momentarily froze him to the spot.

"Oh hell no! You didn't do that." He immediately popped her on her ass and dropped her down, but he didn't let go. "Naughty girls get turned over a knee for spankings."

The smile on her face was radiant. "You wouldn't dare, city boy, no matter how much of a man you are."

He leaned against his new patrol car. The completion of his "probationary" two weeks rated him an upgrade from the piece of shit he'd driven previously. He pulled her to him and smiled. "How much did you hear?"

She cast a glance toward the gym door and shimmied further between his legs putting her arms around his neck. "My iPod died about ten minutes ago. Sometimes it's easier to pretend you don't hear it."

He widened his legs and pulled her tight against him. Over her shoulder, he saw the unfamiliar men still loitering. He glanced back at her and smiled. "How about we go home?"

She laughed and pulled away from him. "Fine, last one home does the dishes."

She sprinted to her car and pulled out of the station right behind him. He watched her turn off the main road and slowed his vehicle, knowing she knew every shortcut and back road in the county. Besides, dishes weren't bad. Especially when she sat on the counter and visited with him. He smiled to himself and chuckled. *Hell, I'm actually enjoying playing house.*

Cole pulled into the empty driveway amazed she hadn't beaten him home. He opened the car door. A blast of hot air consumed the air-conditioned interior of his vehicle. Even though it was June, with the heat hitting the high nineties and the humidity pegged at 85%, breathing water would be a fair description. Sweaty, smelly and hot, he headed straight for the shower. The little water heater held enough for about a shower and a half. Tonight, Bella would have to wait or take a quick shower. He'd pulled on a pair of jeans and threw a T-shirt over his shoulder when he froze at Logan's angry hiss, "Beau, get out! How dare you come back here?"

Cole darted to his room, grabbed his .45 and headed downstairs. He silently walked into the kitchen and stood directly behind her. His left hand reached out and circled her waist landing lightly on her hip.

Her body shook. The man across the room stood six foot. Maybe. His close-cropped blond hair and porn star mustache reminded Cole of a nineteen eighties cop show wanna-be. His appearance startled the man. Stupid fuck. No matter how you add it, two patrol cars parked in the drive equals two cops. The man shifted, giving his full attention to Cole. His new stance showed the butt of a handgun under an opened button-down shirt pulled on over a black t-shirt. The man's body language reeked of aggression.

"So it's true, huh? You got yourself someone? I know he's not sleeping with you and we both know why. Ain't that right, sugar?"

Logan's voice trembled, "Shut up and get out! Just leave!"

The man leered at Logan until Cole flipped the safety off his weapon. The metallic click of the mechanism stilled the room to the point of absolute silence. Vicious green eyes collided with ice blue ones. Cole held the weapon beside his thigh.

"I believe the lady told you to leave. You have intruded illegally and are armed. This makes you a threat to *my* home and *my* woman. Under Mississippi's Castle Doctrine, I have the right to use lethal force to defend my home."

Logan turned and leaned into Cole, hiding her face against his chest. He slid his hand up her back and held her close. A small movement of muscle lifted the weapon which had been hanging by his leg. "Leave now, and if you value your pathetic life, *never* come back or I *will* end you.

Cole held Logan to his chest as he watched the man lift his hands into the air and carefully back toward the front door. He could feel her tears on his chest. Rage burned through his body and demanded he crush the bastard who'd made his strong, beautiful woman cry. Jesus, the south had more than its fair share of misogynistic sons-of-bitches. He walked to the front door with her tucked to his side and watched the man drive away. He'd never forget the plate number. The bastard had better drive like an old woman on Sunday. Cole locked the door and walked them over to the couch. He sat down and pulled her onto his lap. They sat together for several long minutes while he stroked her hair.

"Want to talk about it?"

Logan pushed close and shook her head. "No. I'm sorry."

"For what? Having a past? Having an asshole of an ex-boyfriend who can only feel good about himself if you feel bad? All this is rather mundane if you think about it."

Her response might have been a laugh or sob. She pulled away from his chest and swiped at her cheeks. "No, I'm sorry I got you all smelly again. You've showered, and I haven't."

He chuckled. "Yeah, odiferous, aren't you? Okay, beautiful, shower time for you." He forced a levity into his voice he didn't feel. She obviously wanted to change the subject and probably needed some time to erect her emotional barriers. He wouldn't force her to talk, although the fact that she didn't bothered him more than he wanted to admit.

When she headed up the stairs, he started pacing. *The bastard.* Cole dropped to the couch and raked his fingers through his hair. The son-of-a-bitch had hurt Logan. She could've easily taken the man down and disarmed him. Cole witnessed her busting drug crazed meth-heads and had seen her beat the ever-loving crap out of her sparring partner during hand-to-hand training. The woman kicked ass on a regular basis. But she hadn't stood up to Beau. When it came to her ex, she lost the strength he'd admired. It was as if the woman he knew folded into herself. Dammit. This feeling of helplessness sucked. He should have been downstairs when the bastard walked into the house. Logan. Was. His. The words interrupted Cole's mental rant. *Logan was* his. *His? Oh hell, when did that happen?*

CHAPTER 7

hy did Beau have to come back and ruin absolutely everything? Logan pulled off her workout clothes and stepped into the tub. Feeding the curtain around the rod, she turned on the shower and sat down holding her head in her hands. Seeing Beau standing in her front room had shattered her. Again. All the effort, the counseling sessions and the healing—gone the moment she turned and saw him in her kitchen. He had been everything to her. She almost worshipped him. He was a firefighter. So handsome and attentive. He was everything she thought she wanted. They dated and for a time everything was fine, but Beau had a mean side when they were alone.

He blamed her for his increasingly frequent episodes of impotence. When he was frustrated—which was all the time, he'd lash out at her. He would hurt her with words and with his fists. He sneered that she wasn't womanly enough for him or any man. Logan knew, on a fundamental level, what he accused her of wasn't right. She knew it couldn't all be her fault. Yet, the pain and the memories of the abuse remained.

Four years ago, without saying goodbye and without any warning, Beau had left. She'd pieced her life back together, talked to a professional counselor and tried to understand why he would want to hurt her so badly. Try as she might, she didn't understand. Simply stated, he was a deadly poison. She realized how fortunate she'd been when he left. If he'd stayed, he probably would have killed her.

Logan sat in the tub and let the water rain over her. The pain of the past floated around her like a fog. The gentle noise of shower would drown out the sounds of her crying, so she let go. The water ran cold, and she began to shiver before she turned the spray off and stepped out. She had to pull herself together before she could face Cole.

How Cole stayed downstairs, he'd never know. With every fiber in his body, he wanted to go up and make sure she was all right, to soothe the pain the bastard had caused. He sensed Logan needed time to deal with a boatload of baggage. He stood at the base of the stairs and listened to her muffled sobs. What could he do? Not like he could barge into her bathroom...well, he could, but he wouldn't take away her privacy. He'd give her the time she needed. He didn't think she'd appreciate a knight on a white horse slaying her dragons. His girl was a fighter. Somehow, he needed to let her know he'd have her back when she wanted to take out that waste of semen.

Instead of riding in to the rescue, he shucked the fresh oysters she'd brought home with her and put them on ice. After adding all the condiments to a tray, he opened a bottle of wine and put the spread in the living room. The sun had set while he paced the floor.

"You look anxious." He glanced up at her as she walked down the stairs.

"I wasn't sure how much longer I could keep myself from these oysters."

She chuckled and walked into the room. Sitting down, she poured two glasses of wine and curled back in the corner of the couch with hers. "I owe you an explanation."

Cole took the other wine glass and sat down near her. He shook his head, "No, you don't. It's obvious the guy has issues."

Logan took a drink of the wine and chuckled sarcastically, "Issues, yes…a myriad of issues." She looked past him out the window and released a deep sigh. "He was my first, and only, serious boyfriend."

Cole reached for her leg and laid his large hand over her calf. "Bella, you don't have to tell me anything." Her grey blue eyes showed the sadness and vulnerability he'd seen when she'd burned herself the first night.

"I still don't want you to call me Bella." Her sad little chuckle almost hurt him more than the look of defeat in her eyes.

"He blamed me for his inability to perform sexually, and he took his rage out on me. I was young. I thought I was in love. I tried so hard to prove to him I could be enough. I did whatever he asked of me, but it was rarely enough to keep him…in the game. He left four years ago. Just left. No goodbye, no reason."

Cole's thumb stroked her calf as he waited, allowing her to speak when she wanted. Finally, she shuddered and seemed to physically shake off the past. Logan glanced at the fresh oysters on ice and smiled. "I'm sorry. I'm not hungry. I think I'll go for a walk on the beach."

Cole stood and extended a hand to her. "Good, let's go."

"You don't have to come. I'll be okay." She set the wine glass on the table and turned to leave.

"I want to come. I understand you're upset, but I don't think you should be alone with the ghosts haunting you right now. We'll walk. Talking is optional. Okay?" He extended his hand and waited.

Whether she knew it or not, she was his. He didn't know what to do with the possessiveness running through his veins, but he couldn't deny the truth. Sometime in the last three weeks, while playing house, their cover story had become his reality. He'd fallen for his cover. *I am so fucked.*

Logan put her hand in his and they walked across the street to the beach. The moon rose over the massive bridge spanning the inlet to the back bay. Headlights shot lances of white light through the dark as cars traveled the expansive concrete creation, but the lapping of the water on the beach was the only sound they heard.

The cool, wet sand under his bare feet and her hand in his became a balm for the rush of testosterone boiling under his skin. He untangled their fingers and put his arm around her shoulders as they walked. She stopped and leaned into him and he wrapped her up in his arms.

"Why are you doing this, Cole? Why do you care? I'm your cover. Nothing more"

He shook his head and breathed out a huge sigh. "You are my cover, but I count you as someone I care about. I care that someone hurt you. I care when men treat you like a piece of meat. I care you don't have friends, and I care you cried alone in the bathroom tonight. You are so much more than you allow people to see. You're beautiful." He placed his hand over her heart. "Inside and out."

He felt the tension release from her as her body molded into his. "He didn't see me." Her head lifted and the moonlight softly illuminated her face as she peered up at him. "Thank you for looking hard enough to see me."

The small crack in her voice when she thanked

him was "the straw". At that moment he could see the through the walls which protected her from the world. He saw her loneliness, her pain, her silent suffering. He'd fallen past the point of recovery, right here in Podunk, Mississippi.

He lowered his lips to hers, brushing against her full bottom lip. She trembled under the kiss. He dove into her, his tongue plunging into her mouth. They'd kissed before, but those had been in front of an audience. This? This was all about them and no one else. No case, no cover and no audience to perform for. His Bella swamped his senses —her taste, her scent and the way her toned, sexy body shivered when he ran his hand from her hip to her breast.

"Oh God, what you do to me." He took her hand and placed it where he raged with need. Her startled gasp did all sorts of things for his ego. He cupped her face and sipped at her lips as her hand rubbed against him. The blessed friction of her hand and the denim of his jeans was almost enough to send him over the edge.

He panted against her lips. "You're so beautiful. I need you." He lowered his forehead to rest it against hers. "God we are miles from your house and a bed."

Her hands lifted to the waistband of his jeans and popped the button. "Are we alone?" Cole's synapses literally fried with the implications of her question. He glanced up and down the beach. Not a soul in sight. "Yeah."

She dropped to her knees and freed his cock and balls before he registered the shock of her going down. Her hot, wet tongue swirled around his cockhead. Eyes slammed shut, head thrown back and hands grasping her hair, he released a possessive growl of lust. Her hot tongue laved the underside of his cock and her hand cupped his balls, rolling them gently. Fuck, the woman was going to kill him.

He forced his eyes open and took in the image of her working his shaft. Her eyes lifted to him as she opened her mouth and...*ohmyfuckinggodis-she....yes!* Never before had a woman deep throated his entire shaft but, holy hell, he felt her chin against his balls and his cock down her hot, tight throat. Fuck, he couldn't stop. He pulled out and thrust back in as gently as he could. Logan grabbed his thighs and pulled him toward her. *Oh shit, message received, baby.* Cole fucked her mouth as she massaged his balls. Pure bliss. A massive orgasm boiled deep and hot. A well simmered at the base of his spine before it radiated up sharp torrents of sensation. The best blow job he'd ever...*damn*...

"Bella, you need to stop, babe. I'm going to..."

Her hands on his thighs pulled him against her once again and he shot. The electric shock of the current slamming from his balls through his cock coupled with the sounds of her sucking him off prolonged his release, and he fucking loved it. Every second. When coherent thoughts actually registered, he had to pull away from her tongue. The sensations were too much, and the bliss edged toward pain.

Cole pulled her up and wrapped his hands through her hair. He lowered his lips and plunged into her mouth as if his life depended on it. She returned the kiss with equal fervor, both feeding on their combined taste. Unfortunately, he had to breathe. It was the only reason he pulled away from her.

"Was it okay? I mean..." Her breathless whisper floated to him on the ocean breeze.

He wrapped around her as tight as he could. "Bella, it was magnificent. *You* are magnificent." The tension in her shoulders released. He kissed her hair before he whispered, "Come on, beautiful, I want you and not on the sandy beach. Not a fan of grit."

Her carefree laugh landed like music on his heart.

CHAPTER 8

*L*ogan pushed her foot out from underneath the blanket seeking cooler air. *Damn air conditioner better not be broken again.* A barely lifted eyelid validated darkness in the room. Too early to be this warm...even in Mississippi. Logan tossed the lightweight cover back and stilled immediately when her arm touched the man behind her. Cole. The memories flooding into her rapidly awakening consciousness explained the tropical warmth encompassing her.

His arm snaked around her and pulled her back against him, but his breathing steadied as he drifted deeper into his slumber. Last night had been a marathon of the most wonderful love making she could ever imagine. He'd been so kind, so gentle and had shown her what it actually meant to make love.

Love? Logan closed her eyes and sighed. Yeah, on her part it was definitely love. She'd screwed this assignment up. Once the case was closed, he'd be gone, and she'd be stuck nursing another broken heart. Beau had broken her heart with malice and hatred. Cole's leaving would shatter her heart with unrequited love. He defined what she wanted in a man. The gentle tender love wrapped in a man who exuded strength and could protect her from the abuses of life. Yet, the assignment was a stopover for him. They had no common ground. His future was dynamic and bright with possibilities. Her laid-back life on the coast and his life in the fast lane would never cross except for this moment in time. He'd go back to build his career and she'd continue as she always had. Eventually. After she'd rebuilt and refortified the walls she'd let him get behind.

A loud vibration pulled her away from her thoughts. She glanced at the nightstand and saw his phone light up as the black plastic rectangle shook again.

He palmed the top of the table searching for the phone as his other arm curled her closer to him.

She laughed and rolled giving him room to stretch and reach the offending device.

"'lo." God, his sleepy voice was gruff and oh, so sexy.

Logan lay with her head on his shoulder and brought her hand up, drifting it over the slabs of muscle framing his massive chest. Cole snuggled closer making the caller's voice impossible not to hear. She liked sleepy Cole.

"Son, your friend Samuel called looking for you. I know you don't like us to give out your cell phone number, so I told him I'd call and let you know."

Cole's eyes popped open and he cleared his throat. "Thanks, Dad. Did he say what he needed?"

"He didn't say much. Only he'd like you to call him first thing this morning."

"All right, I will. Everything all right with you and Mom?"

"Sure, right as rain. We're not going to run off and join the circus anytime soon, but your mom has been looking at this cruise, and I don't think I'm going to get out of it. Why in the world I would want to go to Cozumel, Mexico, I couldn't tell you, but it looks like it's a real possibility."

Cole laughed and ran his hand over her hair.

"All right, thanks for calling. Love you, Dad. Give my love to Mom."

"Will do. Love you too, son."

Cole dropped his cell on his stomach and reached for his disposable flip phone. He rolled over and held the number one on the dial pad, queuing up the call as his lips traveled over her temple, leaving little rivulets of sensation.

"Hayes."

"Davis."

"Cole, stand down immediately on all investigations regarding your currently active case. I need you to come in. Bring Church with you. We have a multi-jurisdictional briefing, tomorrow at 1400 hours."

Cole froze and flashed a glance at her. The questions in his eyes echoed hers. The man on the other end of the line continued.

"There are two tickets to D.C. waiting for you. You leave at…" Logan could hear the man ruffle papers around before he continued, "1600 hours today from Gulfport, Mississippi. Do not break your cover. Be here 1400 hours, tomorrow." The line went dead. The call lasted less than thirty seconds.

Logan leaned up sending a curtain of hair over his shoulder. "What was that all about?"

"If my friend Sam calls, my father calls me and I get in contact with my handler. Deputy Director Hayes recalled us for a multi-jurisdictional briefing or an MJB tomorrow."

"What does it entail?"

"Usually it means one of the other agencies has information involving one or more of the suspects in our case." Cole put both of his phones down on the nightstand and rolled back to her. "Which means we need to arrange a couple days off from your grandfather. Since we had no time to spin it, we will say a sudden illness in my family."

Crap. A litany of items flew through her mind at the thought of a sudden departure. "All right. I'll need to talk to Frankie. He'll be upset if I don't explain why we aren't going out on the boat. Let me get some coffee going and…hey!"

He rolled and pinned her to the bed. His massive arms held his weight suspended above her. "I don't think so, babe." He lowered and pinned her with his hips. "I believe there are more pressing items to be worked at the moment."

Logan could feel the moisture between her legs and his hardened length against her hip. He took her nipple into his mouth and bit down on it gently. She arched off the bed. His tongue flicked over the hardened nub. Little tendrils of sensation settled at her core where she wept for his attention.

His hands, lips, and tongue had touched every part of her last night, yet she needed him again. "Please, Cole. I need…"

"I know, baby. I can feel your body twisting under me. Tell me what you want."

She could barely see his eyes in the low light of dawn. On a breathless whisper, she steeled her resolve and told him what she needed. Instinctively she waited for the ridicule and the shame which had always come when she was honest with Beau.

Cole's lips sought hers out in a fierce kiss stealing her breath and leaving her mind swirling with lust and desire. "Oh woman, where have you been all my life?"

He forced her hands above her head. He opened the nightstand drawer and took out two sets of handcuffs. They'd dumped both guns and all their gear in it after they returned from the beach. Some things couldn't be overlooked no matter how horny a person got. Cole quickly fastened her to the headboard. Her mind reveled in the excitement. He lifted off her and ran his hands up and down her thighs. The muscles in her legs shook as his fingertips traced small circles near the apex of her legs. She clenched her legs and arched trying to gain the friction she desperately needed.

"God, you're so sexy." He trailed his hand up her body and pinched her nipples. Her hips bucked and the moan she'd tried to suppress came out a strained tremor. "I've imagined you like this so many times. Hot, needy, wanting my touch. Did you picture it too? Have you lain in this bed wanting me? Knowing I was only a few feet down the hall?"

Logan moaned. "God yes I'd imagine this. This and so much more."

His hands played havoc with her nerve endings, sending wonderful tendrils of electricity through her body.

"Baby, I'm going to take care of you." Logan felt him adjust his weight between her legs. She heard him unwrap a condom and shivered in anticipation. Her hands grabbed the hard metal links of the cuffs attached the bed and held on. He gripped her hips and lifted her against his thighs. "You're sure, baby?" His fingers caressed her labia and circled her clit.

The sensation drew a cry from her. "Yes. Please, please."

He moved over her. His hard, long length held at her entrance. Logan arched against him, desperate for his body.

"No, sweetheart, that's not the way this is going to go. You wanted me to restrain you and to take you. I'm going to walk you along a razor thin edge, Bella. Take you there and hold you and then ease you back."

His lips dropped to hers and he entered her slowly. Every time she tried to buck up onto him, he'd pull away. He calculated his caresses and thrusts to bring her to the edge of sanity. She drifted on a wave of sensation, needing so badly she begged for release. Finally, after an eternity of acute stimulation and denied culmination, she felt him drive into her, the finesse of his earlier manipulation gone. Logan begged. The incoherent babble of senseless pleas morphed into a long cry.

"Now, baby. Now, you can come." He'd moved to his knees and thrust hard and deep. The headboard of the bed repeatedly slammed into the wall. The crest of her orgasm seized her body and

Logan's muscles clenched. Her fingers latched into the top ring of the cuffs attached to the headboard.

Cole draped himself over her and growled her name as he came. Logan seized him and wrapped around him. Something wasn't quite right. The metal cuffs clanked together with no resistance. Logan's body shivered uncontrollably. Tingling bolts of sensation ripped from her core to her limbs. Her fingers rifled through his hair as they both tried to gasp a full lungful of air.

"Babe?"

Logan's grunt wasn't the response she'd intended but it worked. Cole hadn't moved, his forehead still pressed against her collarbone.

"Did you break the bed?"

Logan tipped her head back and groaned. She'd pulled the two wooden spindles he'd attached the cuffs to from the headboard. One was broken in half, the other separated from the base.

"Ahh…yeah. But it's your fault."

"My fault?" He pushed up and focused on the headboard. His snicker and then full out laugh was contagious.

"Well, you did pick the place to attach the cuffs. Not my fault you chose poorly."

"Huh, so you pulling the cuffs so hard the wood broke had nothing to do with it?"

"Nope. I'm a victim of your fantastic sex, sir. Nothing more, nothing less."

"Oh really?"

"Yep."

"So, I should never do that to you again?"

"Oh no, sir. You should do that to me at least once a day. I'll get stronger furniture."

"Did you hurt your wrists?" He grabbed one of her hands and turned her wrist, examining the area where the metal cuff met her skin.

"I don't think so. I held onto the other cuff. If there are any marks, they'd be on my fingertips."

She watched as he carefully examined her fingers and kissed the inside knuckle of her index finger.

Cole switched his focus from her hand to the tears filling her eyes. "Hey now, are you okay?" The area around her wrists wasn't red. Had he been too aggressive when he'd taken her?

She sniffed and nodded. "Kind of emotional. Must be the great sex."

"Oh yeah? I was great?"

"We were great."

"We were. We are." She closed her eyes at his words. He'd probably crossed a line with his last comment. What if ...*oh hell no, Martha. Not losing your man card. If she doesn't feel the same way, you'll suck it up and march on. No harm, no foul. Deal with this like a man.*

"Do you mind?" Logan's words blinked him back to the conversation they were having. She lifted her arms and the handcuffs dangled against her forearms. Her eyebrows rose in question. Cole reached over her, kissing her as he felt blindly in the nightstand drawer for the keys. When he'd found them and released her, he tossed the equipment back into the drawers.

His phone chirped. *Damn, the world would have to intrude, wouldn't it?*

"Let's get cleaned up, talk to the sheriff and Frankie and get packed. We should have time to take out the boat for a little bit if he wants to fish today, shouldn't we?"

He lifted away from her and made short work of the condom. Logan stood and stretched her toned, sexy body. His brain fritzed out again. Fuck, the woman was gorgeous. Her long brown hair, tousled from their sex, draped down her back. His eyes found and held on the dimples at the base of her spine. *Oh, holy fuck.* His cock started to rise again. As she padded into the en suite bathroom, he followed. Shower sex. Shower sex would optimize the time they had. Get clean and get off. Nothing wrong with his plan was there? Even *if* his brain was getting the required blood flow, he was sure he wouldn't find fault with his reasoning.

CHAPTER 9

*C*ole grabbed Logan's elbow and motioned down the hallway, indicating the direction. The trip to Washington was uneventful if you considered a five-hour delay for a broken airplane uneventful. Cole motioned for yet another turn, guiding her deeper into the bowels of the facility. He'd been wandering these halls for seven years. It seemed like only yesterday when he thought he'd never figure out the labyrinth of offices, conference rooms, and debriefing facilities. CIA headquarters was nothing if not confusing. They entered the briefing room and sat toward the back. At least twenty other people occupied the scattered seating. He leaned into Logan and whispered, "This has all the warning flags of one massive case." He lifted his chin toward three men to his right. "DEA." Again, he motioned straight ahead of him. "Homeland and Immigration and Customs Agents." Casually, he nodded toward the left. "If I'm right, those massive bastards are from Guardian."

Logan's head swiveled back to him. "Guardian? They're a private security firm. Can they work on a federal operation?"

"Absolutely, but they're usually so far under the radar nobody sees them. If this operation involves Guardian intel or assets, the scope could be international."

The door at stage level opened and three men walked onto the platform. Cole recognized his boss, Deputy Director Hayes, and the Director of Homeland Security. The man in the middle? He'd never seen him before. The guy stood at least six-foot, six-inches tall. Black hair and wearing an expensive suit. Cole bet it cost five thousand bucks if it cost a dime. Hand tailoring like that didn't come cheap. Maybe private security was the way to go after all. Something to consider.

A flicker of memory from a briefing hit him. This could be one of the brothers who ran the company. Kline, no...King. He'd lay odds the man was a King. Fuck, their little backwater op was about to hit the big time.

Cole leaned over to Logan to share, but Deputy Director Hayes nodded to the agents manning the doors. The low-level suits exited the room and shut the doors behind them. Without a doubt, they stood guard outside the room and kept unauthorized personnel out of the briefing.

Hayes glowered at his audience. He nodded toward Logan and began. "Lady and Gentlemen, this is Jared King, CEO of Domestic Operations for Guardian Security. They have recently obtained information which affects each and every one of your current operations."

Mr. King walked up to the podium. Cole knew he was one badass mother. You could tell by the way he carried himself. Pretty wrapping aside, the man had paid his dues.

"A lawyer in Belle Chase, Louisiana was murdered recently. Before he died, he transferred a thumb-drive to a friend. She delivered it into our hands. The scope and importance of the information contained on the drive may drastically alter current operations for all our agencies. Guardian has coordinated with the respective heads of the FBI, DEA, ICE and Homeland to bring you in.

From this point forward, you are ordered to cease and desist all activities related to your current operations."

Every person in attendance pulled up in their seat. Cole focused on his boss. The anger of having his op, granted the one he initially didn't want to take, jerked out from under him boiled low in his gut.

King continued reading from a card in his hand. "Pending the outcome of a current operation Guardian is running, we have been given the green light to work this information. Timing and secrecy are essential. To that end, Murphy from ICE, Cane from DEA, Smithers from Homeland and Davis from the FBI, will remain in Washington."

The man nailed each of the agents with a piercing gaze. "You'll be working with Guardian, coordinating a multi-jurisdictional response to the information we have received. As of this minute—I own you. You will not depart from this room until authorized and all communication with the outside is forbidden until cleared through me. Like it or not, you're mine until this information is processed and runs its course."

The man's eyes cast about the room as he finished. "The remaining operatives in this room will return home and wait. You will take no action to further the investigations. You will report immediately to the combined task force any unexplained movement of your suspects. Wait for direction from this task force. Rest assured, your cases will be credited to you. The magnitude and reach of the information obtained by Guardian requires a coordinated activity. The reason for calling all of you in was twofold.

"First, it contains any speculation. You have everything we have at this point. Working through the volumes of information will take time. This task force is up and running as soon as this meeting is dismissed.

"Second, each of you who are returning to the field need to understand the ramifications of an errant word or any comments which may be overheard by the wrong people. This operation is being briefed to the Speaker of the House and POTUS in..." He glanced at his watch, "thirty seven minutes. Are there any questions?"

Cole was torn. Having been singled out to work on the task force was a huge coup. There were at least six other agents in the room who could've been tapped for this assignment. It also meant his time with Logan ended without any way to explain how he felt.

The room remained silent. The gathered agents were seasoned professionals. Following orders they didn't necessarily like was par for the course. Cole glanced at Logan. He'd be staying in D.C. She'd be going back to Mississippi. And not at a good time for their relationship. *Fuck, it* was *a relationship, not a cover.* What was he going to do? Dammit, sometimes his job sucked.

Deputy Director Hayes dismissed the gathering and Logan stood extending her hand. "Goodbye, Agent Davis. It's been an interesting assignment." The icy exterior she presented hit him with the force of a cannon ball fired at point blank range.

"Logan, listen, I..." He grabbed her elbow. She pulled away with a slight jerk.

"I'll take a cab to the airport. Send my overnight case back. Or not, there is nothing I'm leaving here I can't replace." She stopped an agent who was walking out of the briefing. "Excuse me? Could you please help me find the exit in this place, Agent...?"

The agent gave her a once over and grinned before he extended a hand. "Agent Thaddeus Long, and it would be my pleasure."

Logan's long legs made short work of real estate to the door. Cole stood transfixed as she walked out of the room. Gone. No backward look, no subtle indication she was upset. Nothing. *Nothing she couldn't replace? What in the hell does that mean?* Fuck, his ice princess sashayed out of the room in her full glory. Only Cole knew. He knew what was going on behind those walls. He'd call her tonight. She needed to know what she meant to him. She wasn't a one-off.

"Davis? You ready?" Cole snapped his head toward the table on the stage and the agents gathered around it.

Duty calls. "Yeah. I am."

Logan walked into her Pawpaw's office at 5:30 p.m. Her ticket had been changed by whoever had bought it and she was on the ground in Mississippi by 4:00 in the afternoon. She left the door open and plopped into one of the two chairs sitting on the other side of his mammoth oak desk.

"What's up? Where's Cole?" The sheriff leveled a knowing look at her.

"That's why I stopped in, Pawpaw. Cole needs

to stay in D.C. His family emergency is looking like it's going to be a long-term thing."

"When will he be back?"

"I don't know. The prognosis isn't good. May have to stay to get everything arranged for a funeral. I know he doesn't have vacation time, so if it's alright with you, I'll do the paperwork to transfer a couple weeks of my time to him."

Her grandfather knew. He understood Cole wasn't coming back and something had happened in the investigation. Something she couldn't divulge.

"You okay with everything?"

"Absolutely."

"All right then. Get over to Bailey and tell him Cole is on vacation for the next two weeks. If he needs more time off, we'll discuss a leave-without-pay status."

"Thanks, Pawpaw. See you." Logan lifted out of the plush chair and started for the door. Her insides were raw, and she wanted to go home and drop the mask. Only a few steps down the hall to scheduling before she could disappear and go home. The knot in her stomach tightened with each lie she told. She knew Cole's only reason for coming back now would be to reclaim the few items of clothing he had at her house and drive away in his SUV.

Well, what did she expect? Rationally, she understood people who went undercover together could get close quickly. It was natural they'd developed a bond. Just because they'd had sex didn't mean he felt anything more than the intensity of the cover. She was convenient. And, after all, there'd been no promises, no words or actions to indicate he'd stick around. So what if the sex was more to her than it was to him? When he'd turned to her this morning in the briefing room, she'd watched the expressions on his face. She knew the minute he realized he'd have to broach the subject of leaving. She'd seen his grimace and the hesitation before he spoke. But the final nail in the relationship coffin? He'd called her Logan. He hadn't called her anything but Bella in weeks. The assignment was over.

CHAPTER 10

*L*ogan escorted Judge Espinosa out of the Courthouse. His suit jacket covered the handcuffs he wore. The sheriff had Judge Sylvester similarly restrained, and he waited in the back of the cruiser. The massive takedown of corrupt officials was a coordinated effort executed at exactly the same time in four different states and three different time zones. The arrest warrants had been hand delivered this morning by an FBI agent. Not Cole. Two sitting judges, four court officers, one social worker and thirteen other warrants for drug dealers, money launderers and leaders of not one, but two, prostitution rings rounded out the day's activities. Every deputy and five trusted police officers from the city were used to take down the criminals.

Logan's cruiser idled with the air conditioner set on the lowest setting. The fan barely blew. What a shame. The judge, accused of murder, corruption and graft, would have to sweat. *Awww... suffer, asshole.*

She pulled a pad off the front seat of her cruiser. It listed each warrant in their jurisdiction. After several minutes on the phone with dispatch, she regarded her grandfather. "Patrols have confirmed apprehension of all but four. The four who are missing are low-level drug dealers. Apparently, they're in the wind. All in all, it was a good sweep."

Sheriff Deadeaux nodded at the cars where the judges sat. "Damn good day. Since we are done with it, you think your young man is coming back?"

Logan put her phone back in her pocket and shook her head. "Nope. He's been gone for almost a month now and he hasn't called. For him, this was an assignment." Logan moved from her patrol car to her grandfather's, leaning on the door ignoring the judge sitting inside.

"Pawpaw, I've been doing some soul searching.

I need a break from all of this. Law enforcement isn't what I need right now. I'm handing in my resignation in the morning. I'll take the *Backwater* over to Florida or maybe Texas. I have my charter boat license for both states. I'll find some work… or maybe I won't. I have the inheritance from Mom and Dad. It'll last me long enough to figure something out. I packed up Cole's stuff. I'll put it in his SUV and lock it. Changed the locks on the house and left one with Meemaw. If you'd check on things every now and then, I'd appreciate it."

"I'll look after things. What about Frankie?" They watched two other officers bringing out a pair of court clerks. The elderly woman currently wearing handcuffs as a fashion statement cried so hard her mascara ran, streaming little black rivers down her cheeks.

Logan waited until the bawling woman passed before she continued. "I've been talking with him. I told him he could come with me, but he doesn't like the idea of leaving you and Meemaw. I'll call. I know I'll miss him, but he'll be fine."

"Hate to see you leave, Isabella." He sighed and rose from the trunk of the patrol car where he'd been leaning.

Her eyes misted at the mention of the name she

shared with her dead mother. "I need to go. If only for a little while." Logan lifted her utility belt and moved her holster back slightly preventing the weight of her nine-millimeter from pinching the skin on her hip.

When all the deputies had their intended criminal in possession, she moved away from the side of his car. Her grandfather sighed and headed for his driver's side door. "I understand why you need to go. Don't make it easier though."

Logan threw him a sad smile, got into her patrol car and cranked the AC.

Logan pulled away from the curb heading to the county jail to process his-honor-the-murderer.

The drive would be her last to the jail. She'd put everything into motion. Knowing she needed to go and actually making the move to leave had been a hard decision. But life wasn't exactly easy was it? If life had taught her anything, it was she was too damn good at the hard stuff.

Cole sat at his computer console in the task force war room surrounded by other agents. They continued to log in evidence and track down leads gained by rolling high-level personnel in bed with the Morales cartel. Two hundred and forty-seven people from politicians to pushers were officially off the streets with dozens more implicated. Each warrant had been meticulously detailed and executed. He'd done a mental fist pump when the judges from Mississippi, who'd been involved with the prostitution ring, had also been implicated in murder. Bastards. But Cole couldn't celebrate. Much larger fish were frying and the task force's operation absorbed all but a few hours of the agents' days. They were lucky to rack out four hours at a time.

The domino effect slammed the agents, threatening to crush them under tons of information and evidence. When people started rolling over in order to get lighter sentences, the agents working the force had been strained to the point of breaking. The sheer volume of physical evidence and testimony coming in against the drug king's United States network boggled the mind. Cole didn't leave the facility for the first two weeks. The agents slept in makeshift bunks in an office adjacent to the war room. He and his fellow agents literally ate, slept and lived the operation since they day they were recalled and assigned.

"Davis."

Cole jerked his head around at the sound of his name. Deputy Director Hayes beckoned him over.

"Sir?"

"I'm pulling you from the task force. I need you for another situation we have brewing in Texas. From what I've been told, it's extremely volatile and needs to be addressed ASAP. "

Cole tried not to show the disgruntled disappointment running through him. Getting pulled from the task force wasn't the reason he was upset. He needed to go back to Mississippi and see if he could salvage anything left of his relationship. He doubted it, but he needed to try. This new assignment would delay the conversation even further.

"What's the mission, sir?" Cole crossed his arms and rocked from the balls of his feet to his heels.

"It's a joint operation. I don't have many particulars. You'll be filled in when you get there."

Cole rubbed the back of his neck. The urge to beg off and ask the case to be assigned to another agent hit him hard. He'd never turned down an assignment before, but he needed to talk to Bella.

"I'd send someone else, Cole, but this one is too sensitive. I need you to do this for me. Once you get this matter taken care of, you're off. Thirty days mandatory down time."

Thirty days off? Fuck. He could go to Mississippi and beg Bella to speak with him. And if she wouldn't? He'd have twenty-nine days to tie on one hell of a drunk and try to work her out of his system. *As-fucking-if.*

"Alright. When do I leave?" Cole took the paper his boss handed him. It contained his flight information and a pier and slip number at a port in Texas. Water access, port and boat. Probably a DEA joint effort or maybe a Customs and Border Patrol operation. Who knew?

"In exactly two hours. Pack from what you have here. There's a car waiting outside to take you to the airport." Hayes turned on his heel and left without another word.

Cole glanced at the paper again. Exhaustion landed a one-two punch on his waning curiosity and then knocked the bitch out. He was too tired to care. He dumped a couple changes of clothes in a backpack, checked his weapon and holstered it, made sure he had his badge and credentials and headed out.

CHAPTER 11

*L*ogan dropped the engine compartment door. The leak in the fuel line was easy enough to fix. She'd found the problem while doing her weekly check of the twin diesel engines. They were old, but she kept them in top shape. A glance at her watch put a smile on her face. Done with time to spare. The man who booked the charter told her he'd be arriving this morning from out of town. He'd paid in full for a four-day charter, so she'd wait for him. Not like she had anything else to do since he'd paid for her time.

In the three months since she'd moved to Texas, the *Backwater Blessing* had become a popular charter boat. The thought of making a living like her dad did sent a small tingle of pride through her. A sense of longing took over as she edged along the cabin on the narrow ledge between the fore and aft of the ship. Logan checked the tie downs on the small skiff resting on the bow. The sun blistered down and if the light sea breeze hadn't whispered across her skin, the heat would've been unbearable. Late September on the Gulf Coast of Texas matched the muggy, humid conditions Mississippi offered.

Logan puttered doing small things to the *Blessing*. The old girl looked good but there was always something to be done. The charters kept her busy. They made money. But most importantly, the constant activity kept her mind engaged. On a good day, when she was booked and working she'd only think about Cole every other thought. On days like today when she was waiting, she obsessed. What they had. What it wasn't. What she wanted it to be—simply everything. Her thoughts occasionally drifted to Beau and how much she'd grown since he decimated her self-esteem. At least with Cole she knew it wasn't her fault they didn't work. Their relationship was a sham from the beginning. The lover who rocked her world hadn't returned her feelings. There wasn't a real relationship to mourn, but she grieved anyway.

Logan glanced at the bright blue fish-shaped clock. Today's booking consisted of one guy who wanted to get away. He said he wanted to fish, but nothing too aggressive. He'd had a rough couple of months and needed to relax from everything and everyone. He'd even requested she not bring any additional crew. The request sent off some warning flags, but with her nine-millimeter stowed up top and a forty-five resting at the far end of the cabin behind the fishing poles, she had no doubt she could handle one man.

Her plan was to head toward the oil wells and anchor about thirteen miles out. She'd drop a couple lines, maybe troll for a while before moving on to one of the barrier islands to lay anchor for the night. If they were lucky she'd cook their catch on the boat grill she'd attach to the aft. A perfect way for the man to unwind and relax.

With her sleeping bag and air mattress stowed up top, she'd sleep outside away from her guest. She'd rechecked the prep work and sat ready to go. There was enough water, beer and soda in the cabin to host a good-sized party, plus she had plenty of food. The fresh water tank was full and her fuel tanks were topped off. The weather was perfect and she was ready to head out. All she needed was a passenger.

How much longer could he keep going? The triple shot espresso he'd ordered and guzzled at the airport coffee kiosk more than a half hour ago didn't faze the cloud of debilitating fatigue. The exhaustion sucked what was left of his energy reserves from him. He stumbled twice on the boardwalk. Evidently picking up his foot was too damn hard today. Fuck, he hoped the mission he was assigned to didn't require immediate response. He needed sleep.

He thought he'd be able to catch a couple hours on the flight from D.C.—until Brandon got on the plane. How did he know the little boy's name was Brandon? His mother said it at least *five million* times. Brandon, get down. Brandon, come here. Brandon don't touch the man's computer. Brandon, Brandon, Brandon...hell, everyone in the entire plane knew who Brandon was by the time the plane landed. He'd like to shoot the travel agent who booked him a seat adjacent to Brandon and his mother. At one point, he felt sure he'd have to flash his badge to stop a mob from forming. Although, to be honest, he wasn't sure if the mob would lynch the kid or the mom. Both were equally annoying.

The pier split and he had to turn left or right. The numbering system sucked, and he walked about two hundred feet the wrong direction before he figured it out. Retracing his steps in the sweltering heat, he rubbed his eyes trying to get them to focus. He obviously wasn't seeing things correctly. The boat at the end of the pier appeared to be the the *Backwater Blessing*. Same color, same size. Hell, it even had...what the fuck? Bella's boat. Here? What in the hell was going on? He walked as if in a trance to the back of the boat. Sure enough, it was her boat. Cole stepped over the side and missed the first step landing with a loud stomp on the back deck.

Alerted to her presence by the sound of the plastic flaps falling back into place, he turned. The shock he had when he'd walked down the pier and saw the *Backwater Blessing* moored in the slip was quickly replaced with 100% unadulterated fucking happiness. His smile faltered at her slack-faced, shocked look. She didn't know he was coming. Damn, what was going on?

"Hey." *Great, Davis, you are one fucking smooth talker, ain't yah?*

"I have a charter. You can't be here." Holy hell, if the frozen attitude she was blasting toward him was any indication, his woman was piiiiissed. Capital P.

"I think I'm your charter." He lifted the slip of paper in his hand in a flimsy ass attempt at…something. What, he had no idea, but hey, he was working on too little sleep and one hell of a shock.

"Then I'll refund your money." She turned and walked toward the ladder leading up to the captain's nest.

"I'm here on orders. A mission." He ran his hand through his hair. The freaking sun was pounding down and sweat dripped off him. Wearing a suit in ninety-degree weather and what felt like 100% humidity sucked.

His comment stopped her. "What mission?"

"Hell if I know. Hayes pulls me from the task force and drops this on my lap. The only reason I took it was because…" Cole dropped his head and laughed as the trail of breadcrumbs became a road.

The road morphed into an interstate of understanding. "Son of a bitch!"

Hayes. Who would have believed it? Hayes and Logan's grandfather were old friends. Mensa buddies. Those two meddling geniuses had concocted his mission, her charter and had set them both up. Cole surveyed the crystal blue sky and laughed, "Those meddling old men."

"Excuse me?" Logan's question drew his attention back to her.

"Hayes and your grandfather. They set us up." Cole watched her carefully as he spoke. A single well-defined eyebrow rose above her sunglasses.

"Seriously? Why are you here?" Always straight to the point, wasn't she? Well, he wasn't prepared to answer, but how much preparation do you need to grovel?

"I came because Hayes promised me thirty days off after I finished. I was going to come to Mississippi and see you." Cole pulled off his jacket and shucked his tie, dropping them on the deck. Both were wet with sweat.

"Too little, too late." Logan leaned against the cabin in the shade of the overhang and crossed her arms over her stomach.

Cole kicked off his leather dress shoes and

pulled off his socks. His shirt came next. Standing on the deck of her boat in his dress slacks and white undershirt, he inhaled a soup bowl's worth of muggy air and nodded.

"Yeah. Look, Bella, I know I screwed up."

"Really? Yah think?" The acidic, bitter disdain dripped from her tongue.

"Can we please go into the cabin? I haven't slept in…fuck, it feels like forever. I'm going to chug sea water if I don't get something to drink soon, and I would like to talk to you without having to guess what's in your eyes. I hate mirrored sunglasses."

His elation at seeing her morphed into cranked-the-fuck-off, but he'd be damned if he was leaving before she'd heard him out. He wanted nothing more than to pull her against him and fucking hold her for a day or two. He was too tired to do anything else. But give him a decent night's sleep? He'd fucking own that hot-bodied babe. He would handcuff her to the bed to make sure she didn't slip away. For some reason the thought struck him as funny and he chuckled to himself.

She peeled off the cabin wall, disappearing behind the clear plastic strips. Cole grabbed his pile of sweat soaked clothes and followed her. Entering the cabin shocked his system. The cold air blasted against his overheated skin. He dumped his clothes and all but fell onto the bench seat by the table.

"I was going to call you, but things swarmed us. The next thing I knew it was a week later and, well, I knew you'd be pissed. Fuck, I would have been pissed if you stayed and I was told to go. And I knew you'd be hurt. I didn't know how to deal with it from a thousand miles away. So I rationalized I'd come see you when we wrapped. But there was never a wrap on the bitch. Morales' organization is so massive and far reaching, I don't know if the task force will ever be disbanded."

"Good to know." She sat several bottles of water in front of him and backed away until she leaned against the counter.

"Seriously? That's all you have to say?" He downed the first water and reached for the second. His mind raced and the direction his thoughts took him sucked. His mentally drawn conclusions to this conversation didn't bode well for his desire to…to what? Have sex with her? Fuck no, ahh… yes, actually, but oh hell...he wanted so much more.

"What do you want me to say, Cole? You told me up front, I was a cover story for you. By your actions, it's obvious the physical events between us were part of your cover." Her voice lost some of its sting, but the words more than made up for the less than vicious response. Those comments hit him in the gut. Hard.

"Physical events? Holy hell is that how you see what we did? What happened between us wasn't a cover. I wanted you. I still do. You left like *I'd* thrown you out. I didn't."

Logan's arms crossed around her waist, hugging herself. She stared at her bright red painted toenails. Cole wanted to take her into his arms, but even in his muddled mind, he knew she'd retreat farther if he did.

"Wanting me isn't enough, Cole. Not anymore. I can't be your convenient piece of ass when you are working in the vicinity. I deserve more than being an afterthought when you finish a mission."

Cole risked moving. He stood and closed the space between them with two steps. "Bella, you are not an afterthought, shit…you're *all* I think about." He lifted her chin and sucked a deep breath when he saw her tears.

Using his thumbs to wipe the moisture away he kept her face cupped in his hands. "Baby, I love you. I have no idea what to do with it, but I love you." He lowered a pressing kiss against her.

Feeling her flesh tremble under his seeking lips, he pulled back.

"Tell me you love me, Bella. Tell me I haven't fucked this up so bad we can't fix it." She pulled her head away from his hands and walked to the cabin door, looking out at the bay.

"I'm scared, Cole. Scared of the depth of my emotions when it comes to you. Scared you'll go undercover and be consumed by another case. I'm afraid what you feel for me is a shadow of our time undercover."

He walked up behind her, exhaustion creeping in and replacing the adrenaline spike from seeing her again. The lack of sleep fought with his will to keep his shit together and night-night time was kicking his ass. He wrapped his arms around her and put his chin on her shoulder, smelling a wonderful blend of coconut suntan lotion mixed with the pure sweet smell of Bella. "It's okay to be afraid, but you will never have to doubt my love for you." His lips found her neck and she leaned away, exposing more golden tanned skin for his tongue and lips to explore.

"Tell me you love me, Bella. Everything else we can work together to fix." Cole lifted away from her and turned her in his arms. "Do you love me?"

Tears pooled in her amazing blue eyes. The smile that split her face took his breath away. "I do. I love you, Cole. I never thought you'd come back." She tucked herself into his chest burrowing her head under his chin. Wrapped around her, he sighed…then yawned until his jaw cracked.

When he recovered, he mumbled against her skin, "I'll never stay away. Your trusting me is something we need to work on. It won't be easy, Bella. But what we have? It's worth the risk." The rocking of the boat registered as they swayed with the motion. He yawned again, this time shuddering with his whole body. What was it…four hours of sleep in the last forty-eight or was it fifty-six?

She pulled away but took his hand pulling him toward the front of the cabin where a queen-sized bed waited behind the cabin door. "We'll talk more after you get some rest."

"You're not leaving me." He pulled her down on the bed with him. Her warm skin against him as the bed sucked him down felt amazing. Holding her completed him. Oblivion via sleep called with a sweet, sultry siren's song. His eyelids weighed a thousand pounds. No way could he keep them open.

He felt her soft hands tracing his face and he fought the coming blanket of darkness long enough to hear the woman he loved say, "I love you, Cole. I'll never leave."

A sense of serenity wrapped around him. Cole pulled the blessing from his backwater assignment against him. With her in his arms, he could do anything.

The Beginning

*C*urled on the crude bench, Tori blinked and fought to keep her focus. She etched one more line into the soft plaster of her cell wall. The added line brought the total to sixty-seven white marks scratched into the dirty plaster. Her mind twisted, muddled by fragmented thoughts. The words that haunted her formed a familiar cadence. *When would they come? When would the pain stop? Is it morning or evening? Will I die today?*

A door slammed at the far end of the corridor, and the echo lingered in the cell. A low rumble of male voices reached her. She recognized the familiar tones. The guards. They no longer cared if she overheard them.

Terror spiked through her. *Please, God, let it be*

morning! Which guard remained? Was it Emad, the day guard, who slept at the desk at the end of the hall and moved only when someone knocked at the door, or Kassar, the night guard, evil incarnate? An uncontrollable shiver rattled Tori's body. Just like Pavlov's damn dogs, her body reacted to the sound of Kassar's voice. Now just the thought of him induced the response.

Kassar had held her head under water while another guard pressed glowing coals from a hand-rolled cigarette into the soles of her feet. The smoldering cinders seared through the ulcerated abscesses already branded deep into her arches from torture on previous nights.

Her screams pressed oxygen from her lungs. Desperate for air, her body inhaled the vile sludge that passed as water, while Kassar held her head under the surface. A vicious grab of her hair pulled her up, choking and vomiting. The bastard made sure she remained conscious. Kassar knew how to maximize the anguish and terror he inflicted.

"What is your mission?" His guttural English demanded an answer.

"I'm a photographer!" Her head was immediately plunged back into the putrid fluid sloshing in the bucket. Again searing agony ripped across the sole of

her foot, and again the excruciating pain forced an involuntary scream and inhale. Just before she blacked out, hands grabbed her hair and pulled her to the surface.

"American whore! Tell me who sent you!"

"Photographer, freelance... nobody! Please! Let me go!" Her cries of innocence had only inflamed his anger.

The interrogations and torture had not broken her. Her captors knew only her cover story. That she maintained her cover story signed her death certificate just as certainly as admitting she worked for the CIA. *No one will help. I know it.* The freelance photography company would be a dead-end. Rightfully, no one there would claim knowledge of her. The CIA would never have the opportunity to confirm or deny her employment; she'd never confessed to working for them. There would be no ransom, no happy-ever-after ending to this nightmare. Death at Kassar's hand would be the only escape.

Her abused body curled inward, longing for a warmth vaguely remembered. A distant rattle of the guard's keys being thrown on the desk indicated whoever watched over her had stirred. Had Emad provided water or food? Would this be another day of starvation and thirst?

She lifted her head from the bench and attempted to sit, biting her fist against the nausea her movement caused. Tori panted and waited for the violent lurch of the room to stop. At some point, a crude wooden bucket had appeared inside the door of her cell. The mere thought of food or water drove her aching body into action. She put weight on her good leg, holding her useless arm close, and stood cautiously. The effort it took to cross the tiny cell had become a gauntlet of pain and determination. The sores and blisters on her feet cracked open and bloody footprints marked her progress. Yet starvation made one hell of a motivator, even for those who knew their fate.

Please, God, please let there be food. Her pitiful approach startled a rat the size of a small dog away from the bucket. He squeaked his displeasure at the interruption and slid his lean body through the bars of the cell door. A small piece of bread and something that almost resembled broth lay at the bottom of the rotted wooden vessel. *Thank you, sweet Jesus!*

Tori pulled the container toward her. An echo of the scrape of wood on stone lingered in the silence of the cell. The putrid smell from the fetid congealed slime at the bottom rolled up to her. She gagged and tried to hold in the sound of her dry heaves. *No wonder the rat left without a fight.*

Heavy steps echoed down the hallway toward her. The noise of the bucket or her retches must have caught the guard's attention. Tori shoved the gelatinous hunk of bread into her mouth and chewed. The familiar pop of pellet-like substances provided indisputable proof maggots infested the bread. She pressed her hand against her mouth, forcing herself not to regurgitate the only food she had consumed in days. Hysteria fought for control of her tenuous grasp on reality. The sound of footsteps grew louder. She limped away from the iron bars and pressed against the wooden bench that served as the singular piece of furniture in the cell.

Kassar, the evening guard, leered through the bars. Emad stood behind him. Fear gripped her, freezing her muscles, numbing her mind and mentally she started to slip away. The mandatory training classes she'd attended called the phenomena dissociative mental ordering. Tori didn't know when or how she'd first begun to do it, but sometimes when they came to question and beat her, she left… mentally. Usually, the curtain of oblivion fell only for the duration of the attack, but more and more, she lingered in the blackouts that protected her tenuous grasp on reality.

"The whore is useless to us! She is not what they said." Emad spat at her through the bars.

"If she is of no political value and no one claims her, the Elders will give her to me. She begs for mercy now. By the time I've finished with her she will beg for death," Kassar responded and glared at her.

Emad's voice trailed him as he turned and walked away. "You have been warned, Kassar. The Westerners value their women. Do not defile her against the Elders' decrees. The payment will decrease."

"The Elders are fools. She is a filthy infidel! An American—our avowed enemy!" The hatred in his eyes nailed Tori to the wall. Kassar could kill her with one hand. She almost hoped he would. Spittle flew from Kassar's mouth as he switched languages and spoke in heavily accented English. "No pay for a whore. They give you to me soon. I have until you die. Your body food for animals."

"Kassar, you are to obey the Elders' commands for the woman! Do not defile her or kill her. Have your fun tonight. Be useful and make her talk. Your reward will be more than this whore." Emad's sharp reprimand in Kassar's native Afghani dialect earned her a snarl and an evil glare.

Tori understood enough of their language to know her captor's patience neared exhaustion. The guards' exchange left no room for doubt—or hope. Left alone, she turned, inch by excruciating inch, to face the wall, and stared at the display of white marks. Sixty-seven days existing in a hell where her only defense consisted of desperate prayers for the impossible. *How would her father and sister react to her death? Oh God... would they ever know?* She couldn't afford the flood of emotion that threatened to break her. No, she had to bury it all to protect them and herself.

The door at the end of the hall slammed shut. Once again, footsteps echoed menacingly down the hall. So it begins… again. Tori knew she reeked of weakness and fear. Kassar opened the bars and walked toward her. He grabbed her by the neck, lifting her away from the wall, and backhanded her. The force bounced her head off the concrete wall. She slumped against the wooden bench, numb. He untied the string around his *shalwar*, the Afghani version of pants.

"No longer will you hide under the protection of weak old men, American whore. I have watched and waited. I take you tonight. They will not know about tonight or any night after this. Nobody ever returns to the stench of the cells at night." He pulled viciously at the waistband of her garb and moved over her. She didn't resist the blessed darkness that pulled her past the white-hot shards of pain.

Jacob palmed his Interceptor 911. The fourteen inches of sharp-as-shit blade flew silently through the air toward the Afghani guard. The man dropped the person he was assaulting. The muscles in his back convulsed and with frantic movements, the guard reached around, pawing at his back. *Shit.* His knife had missed the guard's heart, but the jailor's sudden movement to the right had merely forestalled his inevitable death. In two quick strides, Jacob corrected his rare error and eliminated the threat. Simple applied torque and force plus acceleration broke the man's neck instantly. The guard's body dropped to the cell floor with a muffled thud. Jacob snatched his knife from the dead body, wiped the bloody blade on the man's clothes, and then signed instructions to his men in the corridor.

They'd eliminated their primary targets soundlessly and efficiently. Pictures and fingerprints had been taken as proof to confirm mission completion for the agency that sanctioned the hits. While his men worked the IDs, Jacob had searched the adjacent room someone had turned into an office.

If he hadn't looked through the paperwork, he never would've realized an American fought for their life in the cell across the compound. Chance, happenstance, destiny or PFL, pure fucking luck— whatever the reasons—he *had* checked. The mission wasn't supposed to be a rescue, but he'd be damned if he'd leave an American. *Damned?* He snorted at his word choice. Yeah right, in his line of work and with his past? His damnation had been signed and sealed—a first-class ticket to hell with Lucifer himself opening the door—but leaving an American prisoner? Not an option. Surprisingly, he still had standards.

While his men searched and cleared the interior of the holding facility with efficient, silent skill, Jacob moved to complete a quick visual assessment of the captive. *Oh, fuck. The prisoner was a woman. Fuck!* Training centered him on the task at hand. Alive. Head trauma and right eye swelling. Her left arm hung awkwardly—a break or a dislocated shoulder. One distinguishable black hematoma on her leg indicated a possible closed fracture. Deeply-caked grime covered her body and probably obscured more injuries. The vivid and extensive bruises over her body told the story of continuous beatings, but visually he'd be hard pressed to distinguish the bruises from the thick layer of muck that covered her. His glance landed on her feet. *The bastards!* He'd seen men tortured to this degree, but never had he seen such brutality inflicted on a woman. A glance at the wall displayed the etched lines in the soft plaster. A record of her days? *"A" for effort, "F" for accuracy.* According to the documents he seized, there weren't nearly enough marks.

He tried not to compound her injuries when he lifted her and silently cursed. Too damn easy to lift. Just skin and bones. Far too light for her obvious height. She probably wouldn't survive the trip to the aircraft. Hatred for her captors pumped through his veins as certainly as the blood that kept him alive. Within three strides into the corridor, Jacob's team closed ranks and formed a protective shield around him. When the team cleared the building, Jacob took his first deep breath since he'd walked into the holding facility less than four minutes ago. The rancid stench below had violated his senses. Outside, the team kept to the shadows, and with speed born from many operations, they cleared the compound. Jacob assessed the uneven ground, jutting rock abutments, and drought-stricken bushes. The rugged terrain that surrounded the camp would slow the team's egress.

"Skipper, we've got five clicks to the extraction point. You need me to carry her?"

Jacob glared at Chief, his communications specialist, as they continued to maneuver through the craggy hills using the natural valleys and shrub as cover. Jacob's size and physical condition allowed him to carry the woman without effort even across the rocky and unforgiving terrain. His middle finger threw a 'fuck you' at the massive man. "Take the point and signal the bird we are en route." The big man flashed a rare grin and sprinted forward.

His five-man team functioned better than any proverbial well-oiled machine. All parts worked as one. The squad knew the job at hand and performed it with precise, calculated efficiency.

Breaking down? Not an option. Each man provided essential skills. As experts in their fields, they were handpicked for the honor of being on Alpha team. Elite warriors. Honed and perfected in the art of war. The men were equal parts of the whole, and each would likely burn in the same pit in hell when the grim reaper caught up with them.

Jacob's eyes never stopped scanning the horizon, his peripheral vision alert to any movement as he pushed his team forward. The safety of his men and concentration on the extraction point focused his attention to the end of the basin.

Jacob felt her head rock toward him. He glanced down again and looked into dark blue eyes that didn't seem to focus. He watched her pass out again. Thank God. He didn't need a screaming or crying woman on his hands. He didn't do female tears. Ever. That really had to be in his job description somewhere.

Tori felt a soft touch on her face and heard the drawl of a deep baritone. "Honey, we have to put your shoulder back in the socket." Opening her eye, she turned toward the soothing voice and tried to focus. His eyes were almost a steel color. He had a handsome face, strong chin, and cheekbones. His nose had been broken once or twice, but the irregularity added to his rugged handsomeness. She noticed his thick black hair fell long against his collar, longer than Tori knew a military man's hair should be. Oh… okay… she was hallucinating. It had to be because there was no other explanation if he wasn't military. She reached out and touched his face. Her hand shook as she felt his warm skin. "Are you real?"

In an instant, his solemn face changed as he smiled at her. "Yeah, honey, I'm real. You're on your way home. Doc here needs to set your shoulder. I'm not going to lie to you. It's going to hurt like hell."

Her eyes never left his. "Who?"

"Consider me your guardian angel."

ALSO BY KRIS MICHAELS

Kings of the Guardian Series

Jacob: Kings of the Guardian Book 1

Joseph: Kings of the Guardian Book 2

Adam: Kings of the Guardian Book 3

Jason: Kings of the Guardian Book 4

Jared: Kings of the Guardian Book 5

Jasmine: Kings of the Guardian Book 6

Chief: The Kings of Guardian Book 7

Jewell: Kings of the Guardian Book 8

Jade: Kings of the Guardian Book 9

Justin: Kings of the Guardian Book 10

Christmas with the Kings

Drake: Kings of the Guardian Book 11

Dixon: Kings of the Guardian Book 12

Passages: The Kings of Guardian Book 13

Promises: The Kings of Guardian Book 14

A Backwater Blessing: A Kings of Guardian Crossover
Novella

Montana Guardian: A Kings of Guardian Novella

Guardian Defenders Series

Gabriel

Maliki

John

Jeremiah

Guardian Security Shadow World

Anubis (Guardian Shadow World Book 1)

Asp (Guardian Shadow World Book 2)

Lycos (Guardian Shadow World Book 3)

Thanatos (Guardian Shadow World Book 4)

Tempest (Guardian Shadow World Book 5)

Smoke (Guardian Shadow World Book 6)

Reaper (Guardian Shadow World Book 7)

Hope City

Hope City - Brock

HOPE CITY - Brody- Book 3

Hope City - Ryker - Book 5

Hope City - Killian - Book 8

STAND ALONE NOVELS

SEAL Forever - Silver SEALs

A Heart's Desire - Stand Alone

Hot SEAL, Single Malt (SEALs in Paradise)

Hot SEAL, Savannah Nights (SEALs in Paradise)

ABOUT THE AUTHOR

USA Today and Amazon Bestselling Author, Kris Michaels is the alter ego of a happily married wife and mother. She writes romance, usually with characters from military and law enforcement backgrounds.

Made in the USA
Coppell, TX
30 March 2024

30741227R00095